A Dog's Day of Summer

A Dog's Day of Summer

Rick S. Glowaki

Richard Glowaki

To Maggie: Be it next to a bonfire or on a mountain you made
sure I was never alone.

A DOG'S DAYS OF SUMMER
Rick S. Glowaki

JULY, 1982
NEBRASKA

Maggie did not read street signs nor maps because if she did, she would have known that she was far from the safety of home and traveling farther away with every step her paws took. The pursuit continued on.

Earlier that morning, just after the youngest son of her Family, the Fairbanks, fed her, she went out the door of the house and ambled off towards the fenced-in and forested hill where she liked to do her business. A male deer saw her before she saw him. He snorted loudly which caused her to stop in her tracks and her large, black Newfoundland ears raised in alert. Maggie was half-Newfie and half-German Shepherd. Normally that combination takes the shepherd's shape of ear, but Maggie was one of the rare dogs that kept her large and floppy Newfie ears. Her coat was mostly black, but she had a patch of white under her neck as well as a stripe of white on her back clean down to her tail. This gave her the appearance, from very far away, of being the largest skunk known on Earth.

Maggie's eyes locked onto the form of the snorting deer, and she charged headstrong toward the wooden gate with the steel latch that kept her within the confines of the Fairbanks's land. Despite the incline of the hill, she picked up speed with every gallop of her paws. She had crashed into or pawed aggressively at this gate numerous times but was never able to open it. She would not have opened it this morning except for the fact that the only daughter of her Family had neglected to secure the latch when she returned to the property late the previous night.

The male deer had had enough experience with boisterous dogs behind fences to not be too alarmed at the advancing beast. But when Maggie's one hundred and fifty pound frame crashed into the gate and it flew open, the deer paid heed to the danger and took off in a great leap. Maggie lowered her head and bore down with all of the speed she could generate. Deers, even more than squirrels for her, were the ultimate prize!

The deer was able to effortlessly glide and bound through the forest and the brush, but Maggie kept him in her sight. The distance between the two animals was widening gradually as the chase continued. The great size and weight of the antlers on the buck kept the chase close, but what the deer lost in weight he gained in strides. Maggie's shorter legs had to work twice as hard just to keep up.

The gap widened as fatigue started to set in for the eager but slow-ing dog. That the chase went on as long as it did was a testament to Maggie's determination and conditioning. She was now more than five miles from her house and still in pursuit though her target was getting more difficult to see.

Then it happened.

The deer knew it was safe from the fading energy of the pursuing dog and thus he began to slow his pace down. He saw a pond and decided to gambol victoriously into it and catch a quick drink. Upon landing in the water, the deer knew he was in trouble. The floor of the pond was not a hard-packed mud sediment but rather a quicksand-like bottom. His hoofs stuck and he could not dislodge them easily. It took a great effort to lift one out of the substance, but as soon as fatigue struck, he was forced to put it down again. He tried to back out of the knee-high depth of water and lost his step enough that he began to fall.

Maggie, though very far away and running at a much slower pace, could see off in the distance that the deer was splashing and flailing about in the pond. Her pace quickened as a surge of adrenaline rushed through her system at the thought of overtaking that deer.

The buck stumbled and struggled but finally made it back to shore. Now, he was the one tired and Maggie was full of vim and vigor. The deer looked back to see what appeared to him to be either a giant skunk or a small bear charging towards him. Careful to avoid the pond, the deer accelerated further west and this time there was no gamboling about at all, just pure sprinting for his life.

As thirsty as she was, Maggie did not stop for a revitalizing lap of water from the pond. She instead also headed further west through the forest following the buck with a renewed zeal.

Many cottonwood branches lay strewn throughout the forest floor. Some were submerged or stuck-up, and Maggie was tasked with either jumping over or circumventing them. Both propositions were not only time consuming but also labor intensive. Soon, the energy rush she got from seeing the buck stuck in the pond changed to lassitude. She lost sight of him and tried to use her nose to smell where the deer had escaped to. The water dulled the scents enough that she lost any contact with the fleeing buck. Making her way back to the pond, Maggie bent her head down and began to lap eagerly with her tongue at the pond water. She then rolled around and let the cooling waters splash all over her coat.

She was no longer in any hurry. Maggie knew the deer had escaped her. She shook herself vigorously and let the water spray off of her, then decided it felt good to be wet and continued to roll and play in the pond.

Maggie eventually waded back to higher ground and then stopped, turned her head left and then right, wriggled her nose, but for the life of her could not determine which way was home. She could not ascertain by look or scent which way she had come from. Maggie, not knowing her east from her west anymore than her north from her south, nonetheless decided to head in the direction that unfortunately turned out to be west.

Every stride was a stride farther from her home.

***

Back at home, as Dr. Elizabeth Fairbanks made her way out to the backyard to say goodbye to Maggie before she went off to work, she noticed that the gate was swinging in the breeze and her massive and hairy friend was gone. She called out to the children and they came running outside. Then, the blame-game began.

The youngest boy, Freddie, pointed at his older sister, Giselle, and shouted that it was her fault for leaving the gate open when she came in late the previous night. Giselle, in turn, pointed at her older brother, Julian, and said that it was his fault because he came in after her.

"Enough! I've got to get to work! Go up through that forest and find her!" Dr. Fairbanks snapped, "And tell Dad when he gets back what happened." She then got into her red pick-up truck and drove to her office on Main Street, where the top half of the building was her veterinarian clinic and the bottom half was her husband's Tool Shop.

The children obediently ran up the hill, exited the gate, and scattered throughout the forest calling their precious dog and praying that they would hear her deep and familiar bark in response.

***

Maggie walked a bit farther away from the pond and then stopped and shook one last time to get the remaining droplets of water off that hid in her mane. She then made her way over plenty more of cotton-wood branches that had fallen along with those from American elm, green ash, eastern red-cedar, mulberry, hackberry, and Russian olive trees. As she walked, she could smell the scents of where squirrels and chipmunks had crossed her path minutes ago. The heat of the day was beginning to rise and so she chose not to chase those ghost scents and instead decided to meander down a well-trodden animal path.

After a few more minutes her nose began to twitch furiously as the scent of salami made its way into her nostrils. It was floating over the forest breezes from a direction south of the trail she was on. Maggie lowered her body the best she could and crept slowly through the high grass until she heard voices and smelled those delicious scents even more strongly. Maggie then began to crawl on her belly until she got to the edge of a clearing, where she then proceeded to stop and watch two young people as they sat on a blanket, talking and eating.

"This was such a great idea, Dee-Dee! What made you think of having a picnic?" the young man of sixteen, Scott, asked as he unwrapped his sandwich and took a bite. He had shoulder-length light brown and wavy hair, deep blue eyes, and a slender frame. He was short but the girl that sat next to him on the blanket was much shorter.

This girl, Dee-Dee, had long hair that was turning from dirty blonde to a lighter shade in the summer sun. Scott loved her fathomless brown eyes and skin that almost matched. She was almost a full year younger than him, but in school she was in more advanced classes than he.

"It's been such a busy summer, with both of us working so much, that I just wanted a slow down day to just be us. No rushing. No hurrying. And most importantly, no parents yelling at us!" Scott said, smiling over at Dee-Dee.

"Yes! None of that!" Dee-Dee took a bite of her sandwich and watched him as he did the same. "So Scott, do you like it?"

"Oh my! Didn't I say it yet? Yes! Yes, I love it! You make the best sandwiches! You always have!"

"And I always will, for you!"

He leaned in towards her and they kissed. She then pulled back and laughed.

"What?" Scott asked.

"I think one of us had mayonnaise on their lips," Dee-Dee said with a laugh and then wiped her mouth with a napkin. Scott wiped his mouth with his hand and saw that, sure enough, he had some on his mouth too.

Maggie silently continued to lay down in the tall grass on the outskirts of the clearing and the only noise she made was when she occasionally had to use her tongue to lick away the drool dripping down from her mouth from watching them eat the salami sandwiches.

The fledgling couple resumed their feast on the blanket as the sun trickled through the overhanging trees in the clearing. Once done with their sandwiches and lemonade, Dee-Dee laid her head on Scott's leg as he rested on his elbows. They both looked up at the few billowing clouds that ambled by in the sky and breathed in deep breaths of contentment. Or at least Dee-Dee tried to, as she had troubling news for Scott but did not know exactly how to broach the subject.

"Are you still so happy with me?" Dee-Dee asked Scott.

He laughed, bent down and kissed her forehead twice.

"Does that mean yes?" Dee-Dee asked coyly, knowing full well the answer. She knew without a doubt the effect she had on Scott.

"Yes! A thousand times yes!" Scott bent down to give her forehead yet another kiss. "I love you!"

"I love you too." Dee-Dee answered back through closed eyes. "Do you think you could always love me?"

Before she could add to her question Scott spoke.

"Always! Easily."

"You didn't let me finish."

"I don't care what you were going to add, the answer is always going to be yes! You know that by now!" Scott cupped her face in his hands and bent down and kissed her lips this time.

"What if some things changed?" Dee-Dee asked, nervously.

"What could change my love for you? Seriously, I want to know what? Because I am so sure about you and me forever. How do you always sign the letters you write to me?"

"Forever and for always."

"Yep, forever and for always. That's us."

Scott smiled but Dee-Dee did not.

"But it's easy now. We're just in high school, no real bills or stress, and we both only work a little after school. What if it all changed, soon, and there was stress or bills?" Dee-Dee asked and now sat up and looked at Scott.

Tenderly, Scott asked Dee-Dee, "What is it you are afraid of? What do you want to tell me, Dee?"

She gulped, took a breath, and then reached out and held his hand. "It's been almost two weeks...I still haven't gotten it."

Scott did not understand and just stared at her with imploring eyes.

"I'm almost two full weeks late. I think I might be pregnant."

Maggie listened to them silently still, and the drool from her mouth continued to rain down into the tall grass next to her.

***

Dr. Fairbanks finished neutering a cat and then called home to check on the status of their beloved Maggie. There was no answer, and she desperately wanted someone to call her with an update. She then went downstairs and entered her husband's shop and waited to talk with him while he waited on a customer. Her husband, Joseph, had a driven personality and a boundless amount of energy. That is why he and Maggie were such buddies, as she was always up for whatever adventure he had planned even when the rest of the family was not.

Truth be told, though she was worried, Dr. Fairbanks was not by any means frantic about Maggie being missing. In the four years the dog had been alive, the few times she actually left their property through errant gates being left open, Maggie always wandered back promptly. The time Maggie was gone for the longest duration, ten hours, she had never actually left their property. She was just asleep in the shade behind one of the cistern tanks.

Still, Dr. Fairbanks wanted to talk to her husband to see if he could leave for a bit to help with the search.

***

The wind was sucked from Scott's lungs and he stood up, not angry or sad, just blindsided. He took a step to the right, trying to think, and hoped a change of location from that picnic blanket might clear his brain.

Questions flooded his mind all at once. Would he have to quit school? What kind of job could a sixteen year old get that would pay those kinds of bills? What would his parents say? What would her parents say? What would her father do to him?

"Scott, please talk to me," Dee-Dee implored as she sat on the blanket and saw him stand with a far-away look. The questions kept parading through his brain and would not let him answer his true love.

What would the baby be, a boy or a girl? Which would be easier to raise? What would they call the baby? A baby. It hit him. A baby. A helpless human life. "A baby," he softly said aloud, finally speaking.

"Yes, a baby. What are you thinking?" Dee-Dee asked and now also stood up next to him. He looked over to her and loved how petite she was. He wondered what she would look like when she was plump and ready to give birth, and decided she would look adorable.

"I'm sorry, what was I saying?" Scott asked and blinked away the fog of all of the unknowns.

"Are you mad?"

"Mad?"

"Are you mad at me?" Dee-Dee asked.

Scott did not understand her question. "Why would I be mad at you? If anything I'd be mad at myself for making you."

"You never made me do anything!"

"Well, I suggested it."

"You might have, but it was always on my mind. I always wanted to, every single time. It made me feel so much closer to you," Dee-Dee said and reached out to hold his hand again.

Scott looked down and instead pulled her close to him and held her.

"I love you Dee-Dee. I literally have no idea how we're going to do this, but I love you. I don't know how we're going to tell your Dad. He scared me before, but what is he going to do now that I got his daughter pregnant?"

"You think I should keep it, for sure?" Dee-Dee asked while still resting her head on his chest and enjoying his arms protectively around her.

"You mean 'we' should keep it, for sure, of course! That's our muchacho!" Scott said and smiled brightly, "That's what we should call him if he's a boy, Muchacho!"

"You're crazy!" She hugged him tighter. "You love me so much, don't you?" Scott did not answer, but she felt his body tense. "You have to love me, right?"

Scott then grabbed Dee-Dee and moved her behind him. "Bear!" he shouted and pointed at the hulking black figure laying in the tall grass.

***

Thirty miles west of that forest where those teenagers were having their picnic, Farmer Mills woke up, just like he had every morning for the past two years, well before his alarm clock went off. He could fall asleep, but just could not stay asleep. What was in his soul, heart, and mind haunted him. He was careful not to wake up his wife, Lily, but somehow she always opened her eyes the second his bare feet hit the wooden floor. Her sleeping habits had become on par with his these past two years. It was just the nature of the beast.

***

"A bear?" Dee-Dee exclaimed in fear. The forests there had recently publicized black bear sightings and her father had often hunted them, along with mountain lions and Eurasian wild boars. As a result of this,

Dee-Dee's father had a large collection of guns as well as bows, arrows, and large knives.

Scott squinted his eyes at the hairy dark form that was lurking in the shadows and was not so sure it was a bear anymore, "Hey!"

Because she was being addressed directly, Maggie now stood with her tail pointing straight behind her in that dignified and regal Newfie way. She stood still and stared straight at the two young lovers.

Scott squinted his eyes again, and with a great sense of relief, he identified the species of the intruder to their picnic. "It's a dog!" he exclaimed.

Seeing the massive size of this animal and the unusual markings, he then recanted, "I think it's a dog, anyway."

Dee-Dee wanted to see for herself, so she moved her head around Scott to take a look.

"I think so, too," she agreed.
Scott patted his thighs and in a friendly and high-pitched voice said, "Hey boy! Are you a good boy?"

Maggie turned her head just a bit sideways and then her tail started to wag and she slowly made her way towards the two humans.

"Aww, what a good boy!" Scott said happily as Maggie walked even closer to them. Dee-Dee turned her head sideways and knelt down a bit and examined Maggie a little better than her boyfriend did.

"Not a good boy, Scott, she's a good girl," Dee-Dee corrected.

"Oh, I was never very good at anatomy anyway!" Scott said with a laugh, and then Dee-Dee laughed along with him.

Scott knelt lower and Dee-Dee did the same, and Maggie bowed her head slightly and the two young lovers petted her warmly. Dee-Dee scratched Maggie's ears and head while Scott rubbed her belly. Maggie then submitted to their affection and laid down on her side. The two continued to bestow pettings of kindness to the interloper that let them forget their troubles for just a brief moment.

"Her name is Maggie," Dee-Dee said, examining the remnants of the dog's collar that, through time and tribulations, had become very dirty and mostly scratched off. "I think anyway, I only can really make out a few letters. But it looks like her name is Maggie. No address or phone number though."

"What a sweetie!" Scott said while still rubbing her belly. "We should take her home, and when we have our baby, she can help us protect it!"

That brought them both back to reality, and the sick feeling in their bellies returned. The baby. The baby they were about to have as teenagers. The baby they would have to somehow tell Dee-Dee's father about, while he probably held his gun or bow and arrow or knife. The baby.

But, at least it would be their baby. Theirs. Together.

"Let's give her some salami!" DeeDee suggested, and when Scott nodded, she ran and opened the basket that held the food. She then unraveled the aluminum foil around an extra sandwich, fished out some slices of salami, and handed them to Scott.

"Sit," Scott said to Maggie with authority and she duly complied. Maggie had been trained well and cared for all of the years of her life. Her Family was so proud of her behavior, and she would have made them proud now if they only knew where she was.

"Lay down," Scott commanded, and Maggie did.

"Oh, just give her the slice," Dee-Dee said, already feeling a strong affection for this beautiful dog.

"No, I want to see how well she is trained."

Maggie complied and lay down all the while trying to lick the drool that was raining down the sides of her mouth at the sight and smell of the salami.

Scott then held the slice in his hand, and Maggie eagerly licked it off and into her prodigious mouth. Scott gasped at how huge her teeth were, easily over two inches long! "What a gentle giant!" he exclaimed.

"She is!" Dee-Dee concurred.

The two young lovers, with the possible looming crisis, forgot all of their troubles as they fed, played, and then rested with the enormous Newfie/Shepherd mix that entered their picnic area.

***

Upon arriving back home a little before lunchtime, Dr. Fairbanks was aghast that Maggie was still not safely home.

"You looked at Johnson's farm?" the veterinarian asked her oldest son, who nodded that he did.

"The willows?" the mother asked, and her daughter nodded her affirmation.

"Behind the cistern?" she asked Freddy.

"I looked there like five times already!" the young boy answered.

Dr. Fairbanks was now starting to get very nervous, bordering on frantic. "Come on, let's take the ATVs and scour the woods while we still have a bunch of hours of daylight." She organized her oldest son to go with her daughter on one ATV and she took her youngest on another. She then told her other son to stay home in case Maggie came home or someone called on the telephone about her.

Among her worries were not just the wild boars that roamed around those woods but also the packs of wolves that preyed on cattle and basically anything that moved around at night.

***

The sound started like a bee's buzzing and then intensified until eventually Scott and Dee-Dee figured out what it was. Maggie stood and raised her head high, her tail pointed straight and at alert. Finally, it was seen through the clearing of the trees, a bright yellow bi-plane, probably from the 1930s or earlier.

Scott, Dee-Dee, and Maggie all saw that it was low in the sky and losing altitude quickly. Scott spoke first, "Come this way, I think it's going to land there!" he said, pointing to a swathe of the forest that was barren of trees.

Dee-Dee and Maggie followed Scott dutifully as they ran through the forest for a few minutes until they were into the big clearing and could easily see the bright yellow bi-plane circling lower and lower. As the three of them stood and watched the plane descend, Maggie sat between the two young lovers, and both humans petted her warmly. Maggie loved the affection from Scott and Dee-Dee, even if the plane's noise and presence made her a little apprehensive.

"Woah!" Dee-Dee exclaimed as the plane bounced off of the ground on the first impact but then settled down into a smooth landing.

"Let's go!" Scott said and then the three of them ran the one hundred yards or so to where the plane had stopped and the propellers were now slowing their spinning.

Out of the plane came a person wearing the old time goggles and outfits of the Depression era. Once the goggles and helmet were taken off, Scott and Dee-Dee could see who the pilot was, a woman!

"Hello!" she said with a jaunty wave of her hand. She then exited the cockpit and jumped to the clearing floor. The thirty-something year old pilot shook her head side-to-side to unleash her tresses of blonde hair. "My name is Gracie Moore."

***

Farmer Mills entered the grain silo and paused, caught his breath, shook his head, and uttered a barely audible, "No."

He left the silo, failing to do the task that was at hand. He just could not be inside that structure. The memories were too painful and much too raw.

His wife watched from the kitchen window as he left the silo, and her heart broke one more time.

***

"She's so beautiful!" Dee-Dee said in amazement to Scott when Gracie Moore was out of earshot. "Don't you think so?" Dee-Dee asked while they watched Gracie scratch Maggie behind the ears. Maggie then plopped down on her side to allow better access for her body to be pampered.

"She's not as beautiful as you, but yes, she's very pretty!" Scott admitted. "And how cool is it that she's a pilot?"

"I know! That's what I've always wanted to be! That or a doctor," Dee-Dee said, still star-struck over this blonde vision from above.

Gracie Moore had explained to the two young lovers why she had to make that emergency landing in the clearing of the forest. Her engine was smoking, and the lack of water was the culprit.

"Want me to get you some water for your carburetor?" Scott offered to the glamorous pilot.

Gracie Moore laughed and gently corrected Scott, "For my radiator. The carburetor takes oil."

As Scott ran off with a container for water, Gracie Moore smiled up at Dee-Dee while Maggie enjoyed the pilot's attention.

"Is that your boyfriend?"

"Yes, he is!" Dee-Dee said proudly.

"He loves you very much, I can see it in the way he looks at you. You are very blessed."

Dee-Dee blushed. "I am very lucky!" she said.

"No, there is no such thing as luck!" Gracie Moore shot back. "You work hard, pray hard, and you are blessed. Good fortune is not a kind of magic, it's all about your attitude." Dee-Dee looked at Gracie Moore skeptically. The pilot patiently explained, "Be open-minded, smile, be easy going, don't be tense, and don't give into anxiety. It all affects your decision-making and the opportunities you seize. There's no luck. There's just you and how you decide to look at the world."

Gracie Moore's words resonated with Dee-Dee. Dee-Dee wanted to argue against it because all of her life she had heard the platitudes about luck. She never gave it much thought, she had just accepted it as a fact, but when such an imposing figure as Gracie Moore espoused it, that gave her pause.

Maggie suddenly stood up despite the lovely petting the pilot was giving her. The hair on Maggie's back raised as her nose picked up the scent of possible danger. The dog's eyes scanned the forest near where

Scott had entered to get the water. Maggie then started to make her way in that direction, but just then, Scott emerged from the thick cover of trees holding the container of water for Moore's plane. Maggie's tail wagged as she ran up to him, though she still had a feeling of foreboding as she looked into the forest. She could not see the three pairs of eyes that were watching her from behind the wall of thick cottonwoods, waiting for their chance.

***

Farmer Mills shut off the tractor's engine and slowly made his way back to his house for a quick bite to eat. His wife, Lily, had waved him in and made sure his pickled herrings were on a plate next to a tall glass of chocolate milk, his favorite combination.

Upon seeing what was on the table waiting for him, he smiled brightly at his wife and said, "Let me go and wash my hands first, and then I'll dig into that glorious feast you made for me!"

Lily felt a sigh of relief to see her husband in such a good mood again.

As he walked down the hallway to the bathroom, Farmer Mills noticed the door to his son's bedroom was open, and he quickly closed it and then proceeded on to wash his hands. His wife heard her husband close their son's bedroom door and her heart sank again. She wiped her hands on her apron and tried to make the best of it all.

***

While Gracie Moore serviced her plane's engine, she conversed with both Dee-Dee and Scott. Maggie lay nearby and dozed in the shade of the wing.

"So you have to be in Papillion this afternoon?" Dee-Dee asked while holding a wrench for Gracie.

"Yes, their county fair starts tomorrow, and then I have to be in Fremont the next week for theirs and then Bellevue the week after that for another one. Then, of course, there is the big state fair in Lincoln next month."

"Wow! You sure travel around a lot!" Dee-Dee said in admiration.

"Stunt flying pays well, but there is only a short window of shows that I can do, so I have to make the most of it," Gracie explained.

"It must be fun though, traveling this way to work!" Scott said and patted the plane. "Though dangerous too, I reckon, with the weather and engine troubles."

"Yes, I've had a few near misses, but I'm still in one piece so I can't complain." Gracie closed the hood over the engine and collected the various tools from the ground and Dee-Dee's hand. "Thanks again for the help!"

"Sure, our pleasure!" Dee-Dee said with a bright smile. "And thanks for the advice about pilot school, I sure am going to think about it." Dee-Dee then looked over at Scott with a serious countenance, "I have a lot of things to think about with my future."

Gracie noticed the sudden change in Dee-Dee's mood, "Dee, I'm sure someone as driven and brilliant as you will work it all out. Especially with such a fine young gentleman in your corner!" This made Scott smile too.

Gracie Moore bent down and scratched Maggie under her chin and this woke the dog up. Her tail raised and lowered a couple of times.

"Are you leaving now?" Dee-Dee asked, hoping she wasn't.

"I'm afraid so, Dee. But if you're ever at any of those county fairs, or the big state fair in Lincoln, come and look me up. I'll take you for a ride in the clouds!"

"Oh my goodness, really? I would love that!" Dee-Dee hugged her goodbye. Scott then sheepishly shook Gracie's hand, and the two young lovers led Maggie away from the plane. Gracie Moore started the engine, and the propeller loudly came to life and spun furiously.

Gracie Moore then started to taxi the bright yellow bi-plane from the east to the west and paused and waved her arm to the two teenagers. Then she went down the field, picking up speed by the second. Just like that, she was airborne and heading away. Once she was a few hundred feet in the air, Gracie Moore turned the plane around and flew directly over Dee-Dee, Scott, and Maggie. She dipped her wings briefly, while Maggie barked her goodbyes, and then a minute later, the plane was just a speck in the sky. Dee-Dee continued to wave even though she knew there was no way Gracie Moore could see her. It made her feel good, in some way.

Scott took Dee-Dee's hand and led her back to their picnic clearing, and Maggie dutifully followed. The scent of danger was gone for the time being, and Maggie was able to relax a little though she kept her nose twitching just in case.

Once their area was picked up and the contents all packed away, Scott asked Dee-Dee, "What do we do with Maggie now?"

"That's right, we don't know her owners. They must be worried about her. Should we take her home with us and put a notice in the newspaper?" Dee-Dee wondered.

"But what if she wandered off while her owners were hiking in these woods today? And they're out there right now looking for her?" Scott asked, pointing to the heart of the thickest area of the forest.

"So do we just leave her?" Dee-Dee asked, not thinking that could possibly be the best option.

Maggie did not really pay attention to their conversation too much, as she was too busy receiving signals from her nose again. Her head swung to the left, her ears picked up, and her tail was at attention again. Her fur began to be raised as well.

"I don't honestly know the best thing to do. Not for nothing, but would the addition of Maggie to one of our houses make the other news we might be sharing with our parents easier, or worse?" Scott asked.

"I don't follow you," Dee-Dee said, confused.

"I don't know. I just had so much fun with Gracie Moore and all of this excitement that I sort of blocked out the real reason we had this picnic."

"I know, me too. I forgot everything for a while. All I could think about was soaring up in that plane, away from everything," Dee-Dee said forlornly.

"Not away from me, I hope," Scott countered while looking crestfallen.

"No, never. Never," she said and walked up and hugged Scott. As they held each other, they did not notice that Maggie had shot into the darkest and thickest part of the forest. By the time they looked around and called after her, she was long gone, and her own personal chase had begun. But this time it was not a deer, and Maggie was the prey.

Scott carried the basket and blankets in one hand and Dee-Dee's hand in his other. Both were quiet in their thoughts. Neither knew what the future held for either one of them, nor their possible offspring.

***

As evening came, Dr. Fairbanks was back in her house while her husband took their oldest, Julian, out on the ATVs. She was marinating chicken that she was going to cook on the grill along with potatoes and of course, corn on the cob! One could not cook out in Nebraska in August and not have corn on the cob. Only Iowa and Illinois produced more corn than Nebraska.

Her husband and son searched not only the forest but also scoured the neighborhoods and spread the word among the neighbors about Maggie's disappearance. As Dr. Fairbanks shucked the corn, her radio played a Beatles song, "Yellow Submarine," and she thought back to when Maggie was a puppy. She used to soothe the tiny dog with Beatles songs, particularly the ones Ringo sang. The Beatles drummer had a way of calming the nervous puppy and helped her fall asleep. In between shucking each cob, she would look anxiously out her kitchen window, hoping to see her massive and happy NewShep bounding up the grass, excited for a chicken dinner too.

***

As darkness started to fall, Maggie laid down near a boxcar that was sidled next to the main line. She never found the source of the scents that she had chased earlier. She was unaware of the three sets of eyes that were circling her from a careful distance, waiting for the full cloak of darkness. The gentle rumbling of the tracks slowly increased as a long train of boxcars was coming from the east. Maggie lifted her head but remained lying comfortably in the soft, tall, and late-summer grass.

As the engine rolled closer, Maggie stood up, and the engineer blew his whistle loudly three times at the sight of such a large and regal looking dog in the middle of nowhere. Maggie howled briefly and barked twice in response. Her head followed the boxcars as they passed by, on their way through Wyoming and to California.

Two hobos, and one bo-ette (a female train hopper) were peering out of their boxcar to see what the loud train whistle was being blown three times for. Upon seeing Maggie up ahead near the tracks, the bo-ette ran back into the boxcar and fished out the remnants of their dinner. She figured there was just enough meat left on the bones of the chicken they had to make it a sumptuous dinner for such a grand and probably hungry animal.

As they passed close to Maggie, the bo-ette tossed the twisted mix of meat and bones Maggie's way. Upon smelling what it was, Maggie's mouth watered and then opened, and she began to eat her feast while the train continued its trek towards the Pacific Ocean. Maggie had her chicken dinner after all.

***

Farmer Mills ran out of his house with his rifle and his thick shock of white hair bouncing just a few moments too late, as a fox carried off another one of his chickens in its mouth. The still powerfully-built farmer was so angry that he was tempted to fire off a shot into the cornfields where the fox disappeared. Despite this impulse though, he knew that this was not wise and more than a little dangerous. The last thing he wanted was any more innocent death.

***

As Dr. Fairbanks finally got into bed next to her husband, her mind was swimming with possible outcomes for Maggie, none of them good. Her husband sensed this and tried to calm her.

"She'll be fine tonight, and she'll be home soon. She is too big and too strong and too smart for anything to..." Joseph's words trailed off, some things were better not said.

"I hope you're right. This has just never happened before. And that highway is only a few miles south of here, and what if-"

"No sweetheart, let's not play what-if. No, that won't do us any good. We'll have her back, let's just focus on that." He wrapped his arms around her, and she smiled at the feeling of security it gave her. Despite this, her imagination still raced to places she knew it shouldn't.

***

The feast that Maggie received from the generous occupants of the westbound boxcar settled nicely into her stomach, and she fell fast asleep. The stars were plentiful and the breeze was ample, which combined to make it a restful slumber for her. The day started with a frenetic pace, and she had continued her arduous exertions as she covered an astounding twenty-five miles by the time she set up camp at the abandoned boxcar on that sidling.

Maggie thought of her Family just before sleep overtook her. She desperately wanted to get back to them. Though she did have to admit it was enjoyable meeting the new people, smelling the new scents, and seeing the new sights that today had brought. Her dreams that night under the stars in that field were of sleeping on the back porch at her home while being petted by all of her Family.

The three sets of eyes that had been watching and following Maggie throughout the day were now present.

The coywolf was careful to avoid any loud snapping twigs as he made his way towards Maggie from the rear. The two coydogs were approaching from the front, and they were haphazard in their steps. The coywolf did not care if they equaled his subterfuge, they were more of a decoy anyway.

While rare in Nebraska, the coywolf was beginning its ascendance. Larger than a coyote by many pounds, it would howl like a wolf but then close out its song with a coyote-like high-pitched yip. On average, these coywolves were actually one quarter wolf, two thirds coyote, and the remaining genes belong to wild dog. They preferred to hunt in packs, and if the packs were large enough, they could take down a moose. Tonight they hoped to take down and feast on a sleeping NewShep.

But Maggie was no longer asleep. It wasn't the careless twig breaking of the coydogs that woke up Maggie, the noise of the ample breeze covered up those sounds. No, it was this breeze itself that alerted Maggie to the presence of those apex hunters because that breeze carried their scent to her nostrils.

She stood straight and tall and faced the two coydogs, one male and one female, who were now twenty yards directly in front of her. The two coydogs were not prepared for the size of the one dog in front of them. They knew she was big from their following and watching her through the hidden patches in the forest as they tracked her,~ but now that her muscular frame stood at attention, they stopped abruptly.

The two coydogs separated themselves by enough room that Maggie could not get both of them at once. The coydogs lowered their heads and showed their teeth. Maggie raised her head and bared her teeth with an angered growl that she had never made before in her life.

Maggie took a step towards the coydogs, and then another one. The coydogs retreated and began to make their hybrid howl/yip noise. This caused Maggie to bark a stern warning and then resume to bare her large and sharp teeth. One coydog made a feint toward Maggie but pulled up and turned back while still ten feet away, which made Maggie start after it. The other coydog saw this and made a feint from the other side, but Maggie quickly turned her head in his direction and snapped her jaws with a bark. Now, that coydog retreated as well.

Both coydogs continued to do this dance with Maggie, starting to attack but then retreating and causing Maggie to get angrier and maybe even a bit careless. The result of all of these sorties from the coydogs was that Maggie's attention was directed toward them, and so when she felt a slash upon the back of her neck, she never saw it coming.

The coywolf dug his canine fangs through Maggie's thick coat and struck skin. He drew blood, but not as much as he thought he would. The coywolf underestimated Maggie's size and strength. Though confused at first and blindsided, Maggie quickly adjusted her attack to the coywolf and threw one of her great paws. She caught the animal in the face and sliced part of his eye with her claws.

The coywolf howled in pain and retreated a few paces as his accomplices seized this opportunity to make their attacks. The two coydogs attacked Maggie from the rear. One slashed their razor sharp teeth against Maggie's heel while the other went after her tail. The heel sprayed blood and the coydog enjoyed the taste he caused, while the other was too timid and she never really got a hold of Maggie's tail. She tried for Maggie's tail again, but Maggie was able to lunge at the female coydog and caught her around the neck.

Maggie's large teeth sank deep into the coydog's neck and severed its jugular vein. The coydoy tried to cry out a high pitched yip but there was nothing left of its voice box. Maggie left the dog to bleed to death in the grass as the coywolf made another attack on her neck.

The coywolf went for the same exact spot on Maggie and again drew blood, sinking its teeth deeper into the NewShep's skin. Maggie whirled around, but the coywolf held onto its death grip with its teeth. Seeing a chance, the other coydog also moved in to attack and launch itself at Maggie's face.

Maggie saw this attack and opened her great jaws. With a powerful snap, she closed the coydog's mouth into hers. Maggie clamped down with all of her might, using the anger and pain that the coywolf was causing her from behind her neck to mutilate the mouth of the coydog and leave it to also bleed to death in the grass.

Maggie put her paws onto the ground firmly and then flipped backwards causing her great weight to crush the coywolf that was latched onto her back. This made the coywolf lose its bite and Maggie righted herself and stood above the coywolf and hesitated. The coywolf, newly crushed by an animal nearly four times its weight, faltered for a moment in standing back up and Maggie hesitated no longer and pinned the coywolf with her great paws.

The coywolf howled in pain and anger as it could not move or defend itself. Maggie hated this vicious beast. It, along with its unholy cronies, had attacked her for no real reason except for the thrill of the kill. Maggie was no threat to them or to their hunting grounds or domaine. But in a kill or be killed theater, Maggie was only playing by the rules and now had to do what was expected of her. She finished off the coywolf with a vicious slash of her teeth and a sound of primal fury she did not know she was capable of making.

Maggie then walked across the train tracks and found another spot to lay down on in the tall grass and cleaned herself off from her battle. The delicious taste of victory she hoped would not change her. Her slumber came minutes after her great head lay down sideways in the now quiet meadow.

***

The Northern Feed and Grain had barely been open when Farmer Mills entered with his list in his hand.

"Good morning Mister Mills," the young owner's son, Jimmy Tarson, said through groggy eyes. Jimmy had been watching Mister Mills come into his father's store for the past year. Jimmy had graduated from college in Omaha and was now being groomed to take over the family business.

"Could you fill this for me please, lad?" Farmer Mills asked, handing over the paper list and showing no emotion.

"Harvest going to be a good one, Mister Mills?" Jimmy asked, hoping to elicit some kind of positive response from the older man. That had been Jimmy's goal since first meeting Farmer Mills. Jimmy did not know quite why it was so important for him to get the old gentleman to smile or engage in a conversation, maybe it was a personal quest and a challenge. Jimmy so far had gone a full year without any success.

"That's up to the sun and the rain," Farmer Mills answered blandly.

"Want a nice fresh brewed cup of coffee? Just made it," Jimmy inquired, still smiling and still hoping for success.

Neither his hope nor his efforts this morning would bear any fruit.

"No thank you, just fill my order please and I'll be back in a spell," Farmer Mills answered and left the store. He was barely able to catch the breath in his throat. Sometimes the sadness just caught him like that.

***

Maggie could still smell the blood of her conquests on her. It mixed with her own. Her wounds finally stopped bleeding, but when she stood she felt pain in many parts of her body. Her left leg, where the one coydog took a bite out of her, caused her to limp. Her neck, when she tried to turn her head, also caused her to wince in pain. She yelped as she made her way from her bed near the train tracks back into the cover of the forest.

She walked the well-worn animal trails and ignored what her nose told her: that there were squirrels, chipmunks, and other chase-able animals nearby. There would be no chasing for Maggie this morning. She heard the splashing of running water and made her way off of the trail and down to the source of that sound.

The cool water on her lapping tongue refreshed her. She then walked into the stream, and the waves caressing her body rejuvenated her. The dried blood from the night before was washed away but not the memory of the attack. That stayed with her. Maggie was in a heightened state of readiness now that the forest showed her what it was capable of doing to her. She took satisfaction in knowing what she was capable of too.

Maggie began to walk up stream, drinking and enjoying the sensation of the water moving and massaging her aching muscles and tender bones. Her gait was leisurely, as she did not know where she was heading. The birds in the trees warned the other creatures of the forest of her presence.

The rising sun was warming the land, but there in the stream, with the lush overhanging branches of the various trees, Maggie was cool and becoming restored.

A dog's bark further upstream broke her out of her mellow state. The dog was barking directly at Maggie. The dog had the high ground, and it was difficult for Maggie to see it. She could only hear it. It sounded like a dog that was maybe a third of her size. It also sounded belligerent and aggressive.

Maggie stopped in the stream, looked behind her, and wondered if she should just go back in the direction that she came from. She then looked forward in the direction of the barking dog. Maggie knew there was nothing for her in the direction she left so she continued on her way upstream and would take her chances with whoever wanted to encounter her.

***

The ironically named Sheriff Rawley and his sidekick, Pete, had been carnies throughout the west for the past decade. They ran the milk bottle/rings booth. But that was not how they made the bulk of their money. That came from home robberies.

When they came into a town with their county fairs, they would leave their booth in the hands of a fellow unscrupulous carny for a few hours and make their way through the deserted neighborhoods breaking and entering the empty houses. While the townspeople were being relieved of their money through cotton candy booths and rigged games of chance, these two crooks would pocket any jewels or cash they came across in their vacated homes.

Sheriff and Pete hated nothing more than a noisy barking dog while they plied their illegal trade. They would soon learn that a silent and strong dog could be an even bigger problem to their plans and their limbs.

***

"Hi doggie!" the eleven year old girl holding the fishing pole shouted to Maggie with much cheer. She then turned to her own dog, Barney, and scolded him to stop barking.

Maggie stopped in the stream and looked at the little girl. Maggie's memory went to her Family and Giselle. Giselle called Maggie "my furry sister" and played with her endlessly. Her two brothers often did their sports together and that left Giselle to frolic with Maggie throughout the yard and forest. Maggie missed Giselle and trusted her implicitly, so she decided to trust this little girl too.

"Barney! Quiet! Sit!" the girl ordered, and her retriever obeyed. She then addressed Maggie, "Hi there doggie!"

Maggie walked over and slightly wagged her tail. The little girl stood up from her rock and walked over and met Maggie halfway and petted her head. That's when she saw the gash on her neck. "Oh you poor dear!" she exclaimed.

The little girl then examined Maggie further and found more wounds. "Oh dear, you need help! Come with me to Pa, he'll fix you up!"

Maggie just stared at her and then looked over to her dog who, upon seeing Maggie's size, laid down in a submissive pose.

"Come on doggie!" the girl said sweetly, and Maggie followed. Barney followed respectfully behind them both.

The little girl led the two dogs out of the forest and back to her small farm two miles up the road. There might have been about ten acres of corn her family grew, and they also had a few cows and chickens.

"Pa! Look what I found!" the little girl said to her father who had his back turned as he was fixing the engine of his tractor.

"What is it Aubrey?" her Pa said, still not turning around to look.

"Pa! Look!" she said excitedly.

He finally turned around and immediately exclaimed, "Aubrey! Where did you get that- that- that bear?"

Aubrey laughed and corrected her father. "She's not a bear, Pa, she's a good doggie. And she's hurt."

The father slowly walked over to examine the biggest dog he had ever seen in his life. The father carefully bent down, waiting to see any signs of aggression from the massive NewShep mix. He needn't worry. Maggie was a good judge of character, and Aubrey's father was a decent and honorable man. Maggie let him examine and then treat her without even a whisper of a growl.

For the next two days, Aubrey and her family fed and fussed over the behemoth animal. Even Barney grew to tolerate Maggie, more out of fear than hospitality. Yet they did not know her name. In the tussle with the three attackers her collar was ripped and torn so much that only the letters 'A' and 'G' were still remaining. Aubrey and her parents guessed as many names as they could think of that had an 'A' and 'G' in it. Maggie blinked lazily at them when they offered up the name Agnus. Then again when they tried Angie, then Abigail and then Page. But when her father hopefully said, "Maggie," the great dog turned her majestic head towards him and began to stand.

"It's Maggie!" Aubrey cried in joy. "Her name is Maggie!"

"Maggie!" said her mother, and Maggie playfully lowered her head and then bobbed it upwards and good-naturedly barked.

"I guess that's a yes!" Her father concurred and then they all gathered around the dog and petted her warmly.

At least one family was joyous.

***

Giselle was crying quietly on her bed in her bedroom. The boys had said it to her a couple of times now, that it was all her fault that Maggie was gone. She did leave the gate unlocked that night, but she was sure Julian came home after her from that same exact direction.

Her crying was rooted not in the fact that her brothers were angry with her but in that her beloved furry sister was gone and there was no news about her return. Her bedroom door quickly opened and Julian entered and shut it behind him swiftly.

"Don't you knock?" Giselle scolded him through red and watery eyes.

"I'm sorry, Giselle, I just didn't want Mom or Dad to hear me knocking on your door," Julian explained and saw that his sister was crying as she sat on her bed. "You're crying?" he asked her tenderly.

"Yes, so what? Are you going to make fun of me? Or tell me I deserve to cry for leaving the gate unlocked and letting Maggie escape?" Giselle asked while wiping the tears away with her shirt sleeve.

"No, no Giselle. I'm sorry you're taking the blame for this. It was me that left it open. I came in late, way past curfew."

"What do you mean? You let me take the blame for -"

"Yes, I'm so sorry," brother started to say, but Giselle got off her bed in a flash and was at the door of her bedroom when Julian called out to her.

"I can't believe you would-" she said while she reached for the door knob.

"Wait! Please wait, let me explain before you run and tell Mom!" Julian pleaded. "Please!"

Giselle stopped and turned to her brother. She was always the sibling that showed the most grace and compassion, and she continued that trait now.

"What?" she asked while standing in front of the door. She tried to look as impatient as she could.

"I was out that night with Gianna. You know Mom and Dad aren't that crazy about her," Julian explained, and Giselle nodded in agreement. Gianna was her oldest brother's first serious girlfriend, and her parents felt he was getting too obsessed with her and shutting out his friends and family. "So there was that, plus it was past curfew. Plus, you know they've been on my case about college. I just don't want to go. I want to be a farmer."

"So be a farmer after college," Giselle reasoned, sounding a little softer in her tone.

"I know, and I still might, but if it was just up to me I'd be a farmer and marry Gianna and start my real life of doing what I want to do!"

"Marry Gianna?" Giselle asked in amazement.

"We are in love, why wouldn't we get married?" Julian reasoned.

"But what does this have to do with you letting me take the fall for the gate and letting me be sad that it was my fault about Maggie getting out?" Giselle asked and walked away from the door back to her bed where she then sat down again.

"I just didn't want another fight with Mom and Dad. I was a wimp, I guess. I just didn't want another hassle with them. You're their angel, I thought they'd go easy on you. I don't know, I am sorry though, very sorry."

"They never yelled at me once for the gate thing."

"I knew that they wouldn't, but if they knew it was me they'd ground me, take away car privileges, and not let me see Gianna," Julian said, trying to justify his course of action. "Me they would punish severely, but not you. Not Freddy either."

"Yeah," Giselle said faintly smiling, "he's the youngest, he can get away with anything!"

"Yeah, and she always thinks it's cute! Like last week, when he kept drinking as much water as he could, and do you know why?" Julian asked, and Giselle shook her head 'no'. "Because he wanted to see if he could pee so much the toilet would overflow. That was all he wanted to accomplish that day, overflowing the bowl with his pee. And when Mom found out she thought it was adorable!"

Giselle laughed loudly for a moment, but then she remembered the original point of this conversation.

"But you let me think I am the reason she's gone," Giselle said and her eyes watered up again at the thought of her furry sister possibly never coming back.

"That was unforgivable. I am so sorry. I really am." Julian walked over to his sister and put his arm around her. "Please forgive me. Please?"

Giselle knew she would, she forgave everybody, that was her thing. Even when she did not want to forgive them and wanted to stay mad at them she just could not make herself stay bitter. But she did not answer her brother back, not just yet. She wanted him to suffer a bit for his sins. She intended on making him wait until tomorrow to forgive him. When she felt him give her shoulder a loving squeeze though, she just had to hug him back and declare, "I forgive you, Julian, I do. Just please never do that again!"

***

Sheriff Rawley and his sidekick Pete were doing their usual casing of possible places to rob under the guise of handing out flyers for the country fair. They would walk up to a house and check it out for locks, open windows, or barking dogs. They would eyeball quick entries and exits, and if anyone questioned their loitering, they would smile and hand them a flier and invite them out for a fun-filled evening at the fair.

Sheriff kept his greasy hair perfectly combed, hoping that would make up for a missing front tooth and flannels that needed mending.

Sidekick Pete had very little hair, but what he did have he tried to keep combed over from one ear to the other. Sheriff was nearly five inches shorter than Sidekick Pete, and he never let go of the resentment about that fact and thus was not a benevolent overlord to him. Sheriff made Pete do all the grunt work and berated him no matter the quality that Pete showed.

"Hand me a flier, Pete," Sheriff commanded as they made the turn up the dirt road to a nicely kept farmhouse. Pete was, of course, holding the box of flyers, not Sheriff, on this hot, humid, and sunny summer's day.

They stopped for a moment as they heard and then saw an old fashioned bi-plane, bright yellow, flying low over the trees and heading northeast. Once the plane was out of view, the two men continued walking.

Upon turning left on the twisting lane up to the house from the street, both men saw a blonde young girl jumping rope in front of her front porch. Both men looked at each other and kept on walking towards her and the farm house.

Aubrey was concentrating on her jump roping and was trying to be able to keep going for a full minute without messing up. She never saw the men approaching her from the road. Her back was towards them. Aubrey's audience though, from the shade of the porch, did see the two corrupt carnies.

"Howdy, little lady," Sheriff Rawley drawled through greasy lips. "Are either of your parents home?"

The sun shining in his eyes made it impossible for him to see anything or anyone that might have been hidden in the shade of the porch.

"No, no one is home now, they should be back in a couple of hours though," Aubrey answered while holding her jump rope still.

Sheriff Rawley leered first at Aubrey and then sneered to Pete, "Candy from a baby." He was still facing Pete when the audience that was not only watching Aubrey jump rope but also keeping her eyes on the men approached quietly and stepped out of the shadows with her teeth bared. Maggie then took a few slow steps and was now at Audrey's side when Sheriff turned back to look at the little girl.

He let out a scream of surprise mixed with fear that sounded both comical and pathetic, so much so that Pete laughed loudly at his 'friend.' Pete stopped laughing when he also saw what was standing next to Aubrey. Barney joined the welcoming committee and stood behind Maggie, also with his teeth bared.

"Ah, can you please give your parents this flier? We have a super fun fair coming to your town tomorrow night," Sheriff stammered and was too terrified to take a step closer to the girl. He instead just gently and slowly placed the flier on the ground. The two petrified carnies then carefully began to back away and turned and walked briskly down the driveway.

Once the two men got to their dilapidated rusty white van, Sheriff Rawley had a sinister idea about how to get revenge on that huge dog and also how to solve one of their problems.

For her part, Maggie had maintained her reputation for being an astute judge of character. Audrey put the flier into her pocket and went back to jump roping while Barney returned to the porch and lay next to Maggie.

***

The newspaper ad in that day's morning edition read: "*Lost: A large Newfie/Shepherd mix, mostly black with a bit of white, answers to the name of Maggie. Will give a reward for her return. Contact Mr. and Dr. Fairbanks. P.S. Our kids really miss her!*"

***

Sheriff Rawley was not the brightest light bulb in the box, but his plan did work perfectly. He and Pete waited until early evening and then wandered up the winding dirt road that led to the farm house where Maggie and Barney were still laying on the front porch. Pete carried a shoe box in his hands.

Upon seeing them, Maggie was more annoyed than angry. It had been an eventful and hot day at the farm. Aubrey and her parents had many chores to do quickly because the county fair flier had done the trick. The whole family was going. Maggie and Barney had followed various family members around the farm that day while they did what needed to be done. The two dogs had been laying and sleeping only an hour when Maggie woke up and saw them.

Maggie raised her head and then stood up. This caused Barney to wake up and then he also stood on the porch and watched the two men approach. Barney looked over at Maggie for a signal of what to do next. Barney did not know whether he should bark, bare his teeth, run after the men, or a combination of all three.

Maggie walked down the front porch steps deliberately, confident in her ability to protect the farm. Barney was excited but also aware that alone he could do nothing against two humans, so instead he ran circles around the slow-moving Maggie and tried to keep from barking.

"There's our two friends!" Sheriff Rawley said smiling and self-assured. "Give me that box, Pete."

Pete complied, never once taking his eyes off of Maggie. He was not so sure about Sheriff's plan, but being a toady he had no choice but to go along with it.

Sheriff opened the lid when he was about thirty yards away from the two approaching dogs. Maggie lowered her head a bit and bared her teeth with a growl. Barney noticed her large friend do this and tried his best to emulate her.

Sheriff reached into the shoe box and tossed out two raw meat balls to Maggie, and then one to Barney. Maggie wearily sniffed it as it lay on the ground near her. Barney scarfed his down without even so much as a blink. Maggie looked up at Sheriff Rawley and Pete and though she did not like them or trust them, the scent of fresh meat was too intoxicating for her to pass up. She gobbled her two meatballs down in a couple of seconds.

Sheriff Rawley and his sidekick Pete then backed away enough to not be a threat and to not get chased and waited for the results of their wicked handiwork.

*****

Farmer Mills tipped his hat to Meredith as the mail lady pulled up to his mailbox that was a quarter-mile walk from his house to the street. Ever since her youngest started kindergarten, she had worked for the Post Office. Farmer Mills just happened to be there because he was fixing a section of the two-post fence that had blown down in last month's big storm. He put down his hammer and sauntered over to her truck as she idled her engine and waited for him. She felt sorrow as she watched him. She had four children of her own and could not even imagine... "Here you go! Hope there's no bills in the batch!" Meredith said as brightly as she could, hoping it helped.

Farmer Mills fought up a smile and examined the contents he was handed carefully. When he saw the newspaper rolled up and bound in a rubber band, he got very angry. "Hey! What is this? I canceled that rag a year ago! Why did they send it to me again?"

Meredith was startled by his outburst but tried to muster all the empathy she could. "I don't know, it must be a mistake. Maybe a free trial to see if they can get you to come back as a customer?" the mail lady reasoned.

"Well, cancel it! And don't ever bring me another one!" Farmer Mills said, almost shouting now.

Meredith paused, not sure how to continue, "I, I can't cancel it. You will have to call them. I'm so sorry."

Farmer Mills was mad at himself for snapping at her like that, and he did his best to try to soften his tone. "No, I'm sorry. It's not your fault. I'm sorry."

Farmer Mills turned and began to walk away before she could tell him it was alright. Meredith thought of shouting back to him that it was fine but then just decided to say nothing. She thought that this might be the best course of action due to all he had been through.

When Farmer Mills got to his house, he looked at the front page of the newspaper and upon seeing that it reported on two more farm foreclosures in the county during the past month, he crumpled it up and threw it into the garbage.

***

Many of Maggie's dreams since she left her were about her home and her Family. Her dreams were of the memories she had with them. Each and every one of them was important to her in their own special way. Sure, she dreamt of some experiences more than others, as there were many dreams where she was either being fed or having her belly rubbed. Another consisted of her running with the children up and down the hills while her big ears soaked up the laughter in the air.

Squirrels, dear, and other targets were also in her dreams, and she was always in full flight after them. Just like in real life, she never caught any of them. The dream she was having when she woke up that morning was of her battle with the two coydogs and the one coywolf. She was so excited in this dream that she banged her snout against the steel cage that held her prisoner.

"Hey Sheriff, she's awake now," Pete informed his co-conspirator as they sat under the tent that held their booth at the fair. It was late the next morning.

Sheriff was greasing the bottles so that no rings would ever land on them. "Oh good, now you can see if my invention works."

"Why me? It's your invention," Pete said, trying to use logic so he would not lose a hand, or worse, to Maggie. Sheriff had a broomstick with a dog chain clamped onto it and attached the stick to her collar.

This way, in theory, he could walk with Maggie and she would not be able to get close enough to rip his arm or leg off with her fangs.

"Take her for a walk, Pete, let's see how it works."

"What if it don't?"

"Then you'll be the first to know," Sheriff replied and then laughed at his own joke, causing his unctuous mouth to open and expel much bad breath into the tent.

Sheriff began to unlock the cramped cage that they had stuffed the unconscious huge dog into the evening before. Maggie was too big for the cage to turn her body, but that did not stop her from striking at Sheriff's hand as he reached for the latch.

Sheriff recoiled quickly but then laughed at the creature. Her mouth dripped blood as her teeth withdrew from the steel bars. When he reached once more for the latch the same snapping of her jaws on the steel bars occurred, and more blood poured out from between her teeth and gums.

"What a dumb dog!" Sheriff Rawley proclaimed as he put his hands on his hips proudly, like he was such a brave and great man having trapped a drugged dog.

"Hey, Sheriff," a nervous Pete suggested, "how about you unlatch it from the back and I can ease her out backwards?"

"Away from the business end of that killer?"

"Yes, sir! Please?"

"I don't see why not, if she's out she's out," Sheriff replied and then proceeded to unlatch the rear door of the cage.

Maggie heard the sound of the cage opening and tried to thrash her head backwards, but she only succeeded in ripping a part of her left ear on the steel.

Pete began to ease her out backwards, and Sheriff retreated behind the table that held the greased up jars.

All the while, Pete guided her out backwards and kept telling her, "Nice and easy, don't eat me, stay calm. Nice and easy, don't eat me, stay calm."

When Maggie had totally backed up out of the cage it took her a brief moment to realize she was now free of the steel bars. She moved her head cautiously from the left to the right and upon seeing there was nothing to impede her movement, lunged at Pete with her teeth bared.

Pete screamed in terror and Sheriff yelled to him, "Hold the stick steady!" and further ducked behind the table.

Maggie tried to breach the distance between her and her captive, but the stick would not let her. "It works!" Sheriff exclaimed, again proud of himself, and then walked around the table where he had been cowering and towards Pete and Maggie.

"Thank the Lord!" Pete said wearily, as he was still very nervous.

Maggie saw Sheriff approaching from her left and lunged at him. Pete was not ready for that change in direction, and he almost dropped the stick. Maggie's teeth got within an arm's length from Sheriff's throat before Pete regained full control. The cry of fear that escaped from Sheriff's mouth caused Pete to laugh uproariously.

Sheriff ignored his own cowardice and Pete's contempt. "It works! Now we can parade around with her throughout these grounds and no one will bother us. And we can store our money in that tin box and keep it in her cage and no one will rob us anymore!"

Maggie jumped and wiggled in the air like one of the great sailfish off of the Florida Keys, but it was to no avail. She was caught. She was a prisoner. And her heart grew morose knowing that not only had these two evil-doers won, but that she would never again see the people that she loved and wanted to protect so dearly.

***

Julian and Giselle arrived back to the house from an excursion into town to buy an answering machine for the telephone. Although their mother had done her best to draw up a schedule to have the phone manned at all times of the day and night, there were many cracks in the coverage.

It was now over a week since they last saw their beloved pet. The ad in the paper had yielded no leads. The endless searches on both ATVs as well as on bikes and foot had also come up fruitless. A certain resignation hung over the parents in the house that it was looking unlikely that she would be found. The kids woke up everyday thinking they would hear her sharp paws scratching up the wooden floors of their rooms.

***

Walking with Maggie was still a tenuous activity even with the broom invention, and as a result of this, Sheriff had snuck into the livestock tent one morning and stole an electric cattle prod. Now, when Maggie fought for her freedom, they would zap her into submission.

As she lay in the cage with the steel bars closing in on her, Maggie closed her eyes and wondered what she did to deserve such a fate. A soft, quiet whimper escaped from her great mouth. Aside from when she was a puppy, she had never whimpered. But that was because she never had a reason to.

It was not just her freedom they took from Maggie but also her dignity and the hope of ever being reunited with the Family she loved so wholeheartedly.

As days stretched into weeks of incarceration, Maggie became easier to walk. There was not as much wrestling that Pete had to do to control her. She had lost her fight.

Sheriff was very pleased with his plan. He left the metal box of money in her cage every day, and it was there when he got back. No one dared to go near Maggie's cage, much less reach their hand into it. Sheriff kept the box right next to her mouth to make sure it was safe from other thieving carnies.

The box made her already uncomfortable cage almost unbearable for Maggie. Now, instead of resting her head on the relatively flat metal bars, she had to turn it sideways to even fit with the box there. She would hit the box with her paw and nudge it with her nose to get it out of her way, but where could it go? There was no room.

On the twenty-first day of her captivity, Pete put the money box in like he always did, using a long stick. This time though, in his haste, he forgot to snap it closed.

***

"I really hope I win this year!" Lily said to her husband while putting the finishing touches on her Shoo Fly Pie. She had been entering it in the county fair for the last two decades and though she did once win third place, she really wanted a blue ribbon for first. "What do you think?"

Farmer Mills was licking the spoon that had some of the cake on it. "I'd give you first place!" His smile, though weak, was genuine.

Lily walked up to her husband and put her arms around his waist and held him tight. "We're going to have fun today!" she declared.

It was more of a hope than a declaration.

***

Maggie heard their footsteps. She was licking her paws at this point, having nudged the box with her nose until it was moved slightly out of her way. Pete eased her out backwards like always. Maggie went without a fight. Deep down, though she was not quite sure why, she felt very pleased with herself.

Pete and Maggie met up with Sheriff as they left the section where their booth was set up. They had just gotten into the town the day before and were eager to find some empty houses to burglarize. They started to walk on a side trail next to the midway and alongside that was a gentle little stream. They heard and then looked up and saw the same old-fashioned yellow bi-plane that they had seen at many of their fairs that summer.

"I saw the pilot of that there plane!" Sheriff said and then made a whistle. "She sure is pretty! Blonde and pretty, just my type!"

Suddenly a squirrel shot past them and Maggie remembered her glory days as an apex predator and she bolted after it. Pete was not paying attention, and had been lulled from days of Maggie being docile, so his grip was not very tight on the chain. In an instant his hands were empty.

"Pete!" Sheriff yelled as he saw Maggie gallop past him with the broomstick and chain bounding behind her. "Get her!"

Pete dutifully ran after her. Luckily for him Maggie had lost the squirrel quickly and stopped in the stream to lap up the water with her tongue. Pete walked up to her and then stopped as he realized what the situation was. And that is when Maggie also realized the situation. The broomstick and chain were laying ineffectively in the water while she faced him directly. And when Sheriff strode up she now had them both right in front of her with nothing to stop her or hold her back.

"Uh, Sheriff?"

Sheriff Rawley was too scared to speak as he faced Maggie who now bared her teeth and stepped toward them.

"Sheriff!" Pete said again, too terrified to even move and secretly hoping Maggie would attack Sheriff and not him.

Sheriff then realized he was not in danger after all. He had his ever present cattle prod with him. He grabbed it out of its holster and carefully turned the switch on and now became the aggressor. Sheriff lunged at Maggie and zapped her snout causing her to squeal loudly and in a high pitch.

She wheeled around and tried to attack from the side but he was ready for her again and this time she felt the electric bolt sear her ribs. Again she yelped loudly.

Maggie backed up a step and then tried a feint with a low attack but then leapt high to try to catch Sheriff's throat with her jaws. He stabbed that prod into her neck and she crumbled on the ground and cried in pain.

Sheriff laughed and wiped the sweat from his brow. It was an evil laugh and an evil sweat caused from doing bad. Sheriff closed in and stood over Maggie and raised his cattle prod over her like he had slayed a dragon with a sword.

"You won't attack me ever again!" He swore and then struck Maggie hard on her head with it. "What is the matter? I thought you were so tough and mean and strong? Want another one?" Sheriff asked the prone dog who withered in pain as the waters of the stream ran over parts of her.

Sheriff raised his arm again, and looked over at Pete, who to his credit was revolted and aghast at his one time accomplice.

"How about it, dog? Want another one?"

"Stop it!" A loud, angry, and forceful voice called from the direction of the fair.

Sheriff looked around and saw a powerful looking older man with a shock of white hair coming toward him with fire in his eyes.

"You don't understand," Sheriff started to stammer but the man cut him off.

"Get away from that dog, now!" The way the man commanded and the way the man moved toward him made Sheriff comply

The man bent down and examined the dog and patted her gently on the side of her mouth. "What is this?" The man asked and pulled out parts of some paper from Maggie's mouth that looked both gray and green. "Is this, is this money?"

"Money?" Sheriff asked, bending down and looking closer.

"Why does this dog have money in its mouth?" The man asked while extracting more chewed up ten and twenty dollar bills.

"Oh no." Pete said guiltily.

"What Pete?" Sheriff asked, genuinely confused, but then it all hit him. Pete probably left the money box unlocked in Maggie's cage and the dog ate all of their money!

"Oh no." Pete said again, this time even more guiltily.

"You stupid!" Sheriff yelled at Pete. Then he raised his arm with the castle prod in it and yelled at Maggie, "You stupid dog! I'm going kill-"

In one smooth motion the older and powerfully built man stood, turned, and knocked out Sheriff with one well-placed punch to the nose. Sheriff's head landed in the mud and his legs were in the stream.

The older man glared at Pete but Pete was no threat and so he turned his attention to Maggie. He scooped the great dog into his arms and struggled up the bank of the stream with her. He carried her all the way through the fair until he got to the stage where the pie baking contest was taking place. Farmer Mills arrived with Maggie in his arms in time to see his wife Lily having a 'Third Place' ribbon pinned to her blouse.

***

When the phone rang Dr. Fairbanks ran over to it and answered it with hope. As the caller asked if this is the family that owns the Newfie/Shepherd mix the veterinarian really became excited. "Yes, this is Maggie's family!"

"I'm Mrs. Kang, you contacted me last month about breeding your Maggie with my Duke?" The caller explained and Dr. Fairbanks' heart sank.

"Oh." Dr. Fairbanks said wearily.

"Is this a bad time?" Mrs. Kang asked.

'It is the worst time' Dr. Fairbanks thought but instead answered, "Maggie ran off after a deer and we haven't seen her in quite a while."

"I'm so sorry." Mrs. Kang said and meant it. She knew how much a part of a family a dog can be.

"Thank you. We are still searching for her. And we are still clinging to hope that we'll get her back. Can I call you after we find her and we can revisit all of the information on the breeding?"

"Of course, of course." Mrs. Kang replied with much compassion in her voice. She could not imagine what she would do if this happened to her pure blood Newfoundland Duke. She prayed she would never have to find out.

"Thank you for your understanding." Dr. Fairbanks said and then hung up. She felt more empty than she had for quite a while.

***

Upon getting Maggie to their home Farmer Mills and his wife set up a cushion filled doggie bed in the corner of their room. Although he was never a believer in letting dogs sleep in the house except in the winter, much less in his bedroom, he knew Maggie would need extra care and attention.

Maggie had no recollection of ever being carried before but she did not mind it. Some big dogs squirm and freak out when being carried but she was too broken and beaten to raise her energy levels enough to fuss.

After he laid her down on the makeshift bed Farmer Mills cleaned her wounds and then applied an antibacterial ointment that he concocted by mixing bacitracin, neomycin, and polymyxin B. Once that was applied he covered the wounds with sterile gauze bandages. Maggie laid still and accepted all of his medical ministrations placidly.

Lily mixed in some pain killers with raw meat and hand fed it to Maggie while she rested on her bed. As she fed her Lily watched Maggie's eyes. They were withdrawn. Maggie also did not seem to want to make eye contact with Lily. Lily thought that Maggie almost looked ashamed, like it was her fault that she received such cruel treatment.

Maggie thought back on her Family and how wonderful it was to play with and protect them. She knew she worked hard for her Family and it felt good when she was rewarded with hugs, brushing out her coat, and an abundance of food and water. 'What was my crime, what did I do wrong?' Maggie kept wondering as Farmer Mills and his wife tried to heal her outside wounds.

***

Mr. and Dr. Fairbanks decided to widen the scope of their searches for their beloved Maggie. They took out newspaper ads in four more of the bordering counties. They, and their children, continued to plaster Maggie's picture on telephone poles along with a phone number and a reward amount, now up to $2000, for the return of their four legged family member. Anytime a family member came home they immediately ran to the answering machine hoping against hope for a message that someone indeed found their treasured dog.

Joseph Fairbanks could not stop walking past Maggie's bed and expecting to find his large adventure buddy laying there. He loved when he would enter the kitchen where her bed was located, and she would instantly rise and make a beeline for the door hoping he was taking her hiking or running. And at nights by the bonfire, when all the others went inside because of mosquitos or just plain being sleepy, Maggie would stay by his side keeping him from ever feeling alone.

Joseph Fairbanks knew how much his wife and children missed their Maggie and how much that dog meant to them, he just never fully realized how much she meant to him until she was gone.

***

The next morning Farmer Mills took off Maggie's bandages and then redressed the wounds as Lily prepared the dog a sumptuous breakfast feast. His tough, callous hands were gentle with the dog's wounds and Maggie felt like maybe she was loved again. She knew enough about what happened at the creek next to the fair that this man saved her life and that she owed him her loyalty, but she also felt like she wanted to share her love too.

As he worked on the gash around her ribs, Maggie gently rested her large head on his leg. He looked at her like he was examining a new brand of corn seed, really studying her face and eyes. He felt the love she was trying to share. But thinking he was unworthy, he reapplied the gauze bandage and stood up causing her head to leave his leg and rest in the air. She looked at him quizzically, wondering again what she might have done wrong.

Farmer Mills paused and debated whether to pet Maggie, but then walked away and left the bedroom for the kitchen. "She's ready to eat, darling." he said to his wife Lily. Farmer Mills then went out to start his day of farming while his wife tended to the recovering dog. Lily reveled in the role of caretaker. It was who she loved being. It had been awhile since anyone let her care for them.

***

As Gracie Moore circled yet another small rural town in Nebraska she thought of how beautiful everything seemed from up high. Sometimes the beauty carried over on closer inspection, sometimes not. For the past month her thoughts kept going back to that bucolic little forest clearing when she had to land due to an overheated engine. The two young lovers and that massive dog Maggie were never far from her wandering thoughts as she careened off of the clouds.

Gracie thought of a question the young girl, Dee-Dee, had asked her when her boyfriend Scott went to fetch water in the forest and Maggie dutifully followed him.

Dee-Dee was hesitant but Gracie could tell there was something important on the young girl's mind. "Go ahead, ask me, Dee-Dee, I won't bite!" Gracie said with a warm smile that she hoped would put the young girl at ease.

Dee-Dee could not explain why but she felt both safe and close to this person who just an hour ago was a complete stranger to her. Sometimes life is like that, you can tell secrets or express fears to someone you have had no past with whereas you might hide those facts or concerns with a sibling or other family member. Dee-Dee felt like she could confide anything to Gracie Moore and trust her to give her sound advice or guidance.

"Well, I was wondering, you know a lot of pilots, right?" Gracie nodded that she did. "Well, and you know a lot of female pilots too, right?"

"Not that many. There are not a lot of us out there." Gracie explained.

"Oh." Dee-Dee said with a dejected tone. "But of the few you know, did any of them have children before they became pilots?"

"Do you mean they were moms?" Gracie asked.

"Yes. And if so, were any of them moms when they were really young?" Dee-Dee asked nervously while looking back at the forest to make sure Scott was not coming back yet with the water. Dee-Dee was afraid Scott might not want her telling Gracie Moore about their possible situation.

"Really young?"

"Yes, like, I don't know, fifteen or sixteen or so." Dee-Dee sheepishly said and then Gracie understood all too well.

"If a girl has a man that loves her completely and unselfishly, then she can accomplish anything she sets her mind to." Gracie said and then was rewarded with a beaming smile from Dee-Dee, and then a genuine hug.

Gracie wondered what happened to that young couple and if what they feared came true or not.

Thinking of Dee-Dee made Gracie ponder back on her younger days. At first she wanted to be a professional tennis player and marry Bjorn Borg. Then she wanted to be a dermatologist in a small town in North Carolina. Then Gracie wanted to just be a mom and be married to a doctor. Finally Gracie decided she wanted to be a pilot after her Grandpa and his buddy took her up in an old fashioned bi-plane. She was hooked!

With her Grandpa financing it, she entered flight school and by the time Gracie turned twenty-three she was fully licensed. The next summer she set out for Alaska and became a bush pilot ferrying fishermen to remote cabins and landing her pontoon planes onto pristine lakes.

In the late summer and early fall she started to do stunt flying at county and state fairs throughout the lower forty-eight. It was an exciting life that she treasured. Sure, sometimes she longed for stability : a home, a husband, children, a normal life. But for now she wanted to push her personal limits.

Her father thought she was foolish and reckless to be doing such a dangerous job. "You're smart, so driven, why not be a lawyer with me? You could make partner at my firm in no time!"

"That's just not me, Daddy." Gracie would explain to her father as he harrumphed around the room in agitation. "I don't want to be at a desk, or indoors, or tied down. Not yet, anyway. Maybe someday, just not yet." Her mother looked on with envy at Gracie and said very little when her husband was around. Privately she often stroked her daughter's hair and kept telling her to live out her dreams.

Along with thoughts of her Grandpa, her parents, and Dee-Dee and Scott, Gracie wondered if that massive and sweet dog Maggie ever found her way back to her Family. As she flew over Nebraska on that beautiful summer's afternoon while she headed to the state fair, Gracie loved to peer down at the farms with their congruent rows of corn that waved with every breeze that blew. No, she thought, she did not want to be at a desk, indoors, chained down.

***

Farmer Mills surprised himself by taking Maggie with him into town to pick up supplies at the Northern Feed and Grain Store. He surely surprised his wife Lily, "You are?" She asked him when he told her his plans. "Well, that's quite a nice surprise, you'll really make her day!" Lily added. Lily had noticed how Maggie had tried repeatedly to bestow the love that she felt but Farmer Mills just did not accept love or affection easily, anymore.

When Maggie would rest her head on Farmer Mills leg he would suddenly remember somewhere else he had to be and would rise and walk away. When Maggie would wag her tail and eagerly stride toward Farmer Mills in the morning as he came through the hallway to the kitchen for breakfast, he would see her and break away instead to the bathroom. Lily also would see that sometimes he would begin to pet her but then would be self-conscious of it and abruptly stop. His wife knew why her husband acted this way, but she hoped he would heal and somehow move on. The walls he had constructed, though, were formidable.

"Dog food? You want dog food?" Jimmy Tarson asked excitedly. "When did you get a dog? What kind? Is it a boy or girl? Is it a puppy?"

Farmer Mills let Jimmy rattle off his litany of questions and just stared at him until the boy quieted down. "You should work for the newspaper the way you interview people."

"Just kind of surprised me, that's all." Jimmy said, never losing his smile. Maybe that was why Farmer Mills was so taken aback whenever he dealt with Jimmy : the perpetual smile and the general excitement about life made him seem very familiar.

"We found her at the county fair. She was being abused. I stopped the men from hurting her and took her home and we're mending her."

"Wow! Good for you, sir! Poor doggie! Can I meet her someday?"

"She's in the truck now, if you like." Farmer Mills said while pointing his thumb backwards out of the store and into the parking lot.

Jimmy walked out of the door and through the parking lot to the pick-up truck he knew was Farmer Mills's. Sitting in the passenger seat was the biggest and most unique dog he ever saw. Maggie stared at the man and never blinked while making eye contact. Maggie thought he looked like a peaceful soul but then again her duty was to protect Farmer Mills's pick-up truck so...

Jimmy wanted to pet her but then thought better of it. He ran back to the store and found Farmer Mills eyeing some doggie treats. "That's no dog! That's a BearWolf!"

Farmer Mills actually let out a laugh. Jimmy had never heard him laugh before. It sounded good. Deep and yet light at the same time.

"She's pretty friendly." Farmer Mills assured the young man.

"I didn't get close enough to find out!"

"Come on, I'll show you." Jimmy was amazed that Farmer Mills was taking time for him and actually engaging into conversation.

"Sure, if you say so!" Jimmy responded and followed the farmer as he walked out to his pickup truck and opened the passenger door. Maggie came bounding out with her tail wagging and greeted Farmer Mills like they hadn't seen each other in years. Jimmy watched this display of affection from the dog to the man. "She sure loves her daddy!"

Farmer Mills' face turned cold, "I'm nobody's daddy! Not hers, and she's not ours, I just helped her out of a jam."

"Oh, I know, I know -" Jimmy stammered, mad at himself for upsetting the farmer just when he finally was making some headway with him.

"When the owners come by to get her, off she'll go. She'll leave." Farmer Mills sounded like he was dreading that outcome.

Jimmy was not sure what to say at this point. "Well, she sure is enjoying you until they do."

Farmer Mills looked at Maggie as she sat on his foot and tilted her great head so he just had to pet her. And he did.

Jimmy watched the old man scratch the dog behind her ears affectionately and now felt bold enough to add, "And I think you're enjoying her too."

On the truck ride back Maggie sat with her great head sticking out of the open window and reminisced upon her times doing that in her Family's truck. The Fairbanks also had a pickup truck along with a 1981 Ford Bronco.

Maggie was always excited when the call came to get into either vehicle because it meant an adventure with whichever family member was accompanying her. She was a well behaved passenger and made it easy for whomever drove her. She would look at other dogs that were walking down the street with their owners while she rode by with hers and felt superior. She knew those other dogs envied her and her Family.

They were the only people she had ever known. Dr. Fairbanks acquired her as payment just after she was born in a litter that numbered five. Shortly after, the family that used Maggie as currency, lost their farm to foreclosure. It was a fate that was happening more and more as the late 1970's gave way to the early 1980's.

Upon bringing her home Dr. Fairbanks had to patiently explain to Giselle that the little girl could not have the puppy sleep in the bed with her.

"But I won't crush her, Mom, I promise!" Giselle said.

As a veterinarian Dr. Fairbanks knew that was just one of many reasons a two month old puppy should not sleep in her daughter's bed. But the mother let the daughter setup accommodations for the tiny fur ball of a dog. The two boys helped as well, it was truly a family affair.

Soon Maggie was growing quickly and surprised everyone with her increasing weight and height. She was the pick of the litter.

By four months she was running wild with the boys in the forest and while napping Giselle would dress her up in her clothes.

Mr. and Dr. Fairbanks loved the extra protection Maggie provided because as she grew to her full weight of one hundred and fifty pounds she was a worthy adversary of any man or beast in the area. Maggie was never mean spirited to strangers, but her presence was enough of a warning and her bark, though used sparingly, was nearly window rattling in its power and volume.

As Maggie rode in the pickup truck back from the store with Farmer Mills she was eager to see her Family again, but until that time, she was going to love the man who rescued her as much as he decided he would let her.

***

Upon leaving the pickup truck once they got back to the farmhouse from the feed and grain store, Maggie wagged her tail and greeted Farmer Mills' wife. Maggie proceeded to sit on Lily's foot and waited for the weathered hands of the beautiful old farmer's wife to pet her vigorously, which the lady did. Maggie then ran over to the chicken coop and sent them flying about with one of her rare barks. Maggie did it out of a playful want to see those funny looking feathered creatures fly to and from at her instigation.

Both Farmer Mills and his wife laughed loudly at the sight of the great beast causing so much commotion. "I bet they're not going to miss her when her owners come for her." The farmer said and his wife suddenly became sad.

"I sure am."

"I know you will, honey."

"You will too, if you want to be honest with yourself!" She said in an almost scolding tone, but masked it with a smile.

"Did you put the ad in the paper about her?"

"I did."

"Good. They probably miss her very much."

"Yes. Just like we will." Lily said and turned and walked back into the farm house.

***

After dinner Farmer Mills and his wife Lily swayed on the loveseat rocking chair that hung from the front porch ceiling while Maggie draped her huge paws over the top step and rested her great head on her forearms. The air was still and the sky was clear. The temperature was idyllic for relaxing after a filling meal. It was a prime moment for introspection and contemplation and that is what made Farmer Mills get antsy. It was too quiet. Too still.

He felt like he should have a conversation with his wife but did not know what to say. He looked over to her and she was gazing up at the stars with a slight smile. He thought she looked like she might be in the middle of a prayer. Her countenance was peaceful but yet searching. He could not quite describe it. Looking at her though, in the starlight, he knew for a fact he loved her deeply. He thought that might be a nice thing to say to break the silence.

"Lily," Farmer Mills started to say to his wife but then Maggie's great head lifted quickly and a quiet growl escaped from her mouth. Farmer Mills' attention was drawn to the darkness and what might be peaking Maggie's interest. It was a dark sea of corn stalks that gently waved before them on the front porch of the farm house. The waning gibbous moon of that early September sky provided illumination but the passing clouds intermittently dimmed the light.

"What? Dear?" Lily asked her husband.

"Whatever got her worked up she either sniffed or heard, there ain't nothing to see in that corn field tonight with these clouds." Farmer Mills commented to his wife while nonetheless staring out into the darkness, hoping against hope he could catch a glance at what Maggie was agitated about.

A brown/reddish form made its way to the fence of the chicken coop and Maggie rose and was off of the porch in a blur. "A fox!" Farmer Mills said with a yell while pointing in the direction of the chicken coop. Maggie's sharp nails on the wooden porch made enough noise to warn and scare the fox before the dog was even on the dirt pathway to the coop.

"Go get 'em, girl!" Farmer Mills yelled encouragingly to Maggie who was already hot on the chase of the fox through the corn field. Both the farmer and his wife stood and tried to tell where the chase was leading. They could see several stalks being knocked over by the zealous and cumbersome dog.

"Do you think she'll catch it?" His wife asked him.

"If any dog could, it'd be her." Farmer Mills said and his wife could tell he was thrilled at the prospect of Maggie catching that murderous fox.

Eventually they noticed that the direction of the pattern of stalks being knocked down no longer were being pushed away from the house; they now seemed to be falling back toward the farm house. The fox eluded Maggie and now the dog was returning defeated.

When the couple saw the dog they expected her to rejoin them on the porch and rest from her sprint, but instead, she walked over to the chicken coop and stopped. The farmer and his wife watched her sniff the air and feel the breeze, she then went to the eastern side of the coop and lay down in the darkness of the overhang where she was unable to be seen. "Well what do you suppose she's doing there?" Lily asked her husband but he just shook his head and shrugged his shoulders.

They couple stayed and swung a while longer and then went inside the house to get ready for bed. They had been inside for nearly an hour when suddenly they heard a high pierced shriek from near the chicken coop. They both ran outside in time to see Maggie with her fangs deep in the foxes neck and then she violently shook the fox and all was quiet. With the fox still in her mouth and it's warm blood slowly running down her throat she walked a couple of steps towards the front porch and dropped the carcass of the chicken killer.

The farmer and his wife were mightily impressed with Maggie and this time Farmer Mills held nothing back in his affection for her, "Come here, girl!" He said, as they still did not know her name, and petted her strongly behind her ears. She plopped down sideways and now he also petted her belly.

His wife was shocked at the amount of love her husband seemed to finally pour out to the dog. When he looked over at his wife and saw the look of astonishment on her face over his level of open affection Farmer Mills became self-conscious and stopped petting Maggie. He stood up and straightened his pants and turned and began to walk up the porch steps. "Come on, girl."

"Are you talking to me or the dog?" Lily wryly asked and the farmer stopped and let out a laugh.

"Both."

Maggie felt almost vainglorious in her achievements of catching and killing the fox. As Farmer Mills noted she made sure she was upwind and out of sight for the foxes return so as not to be detected.

Farmer Mills walked ahead and held the door open for both of them and once they entered the house he bolted it up tight and turned out the porch light.

***

The next morning all three living creatures in that farm house arose to a misty morning that had a welcome coolness to it. The first week of September was in full swing and a marked lower change in the levels of heat and humidity were noticeable and appreciated. As Lily made the coffee for her and her husband, he let Maggie out of the front door and then followed her outside onto the front porch.

Maggie looked back at the white haired farmer and then proceeded to jog confidently to the forest's edge past the eastern part of the corn-fields. Farmer Mills watched her briefly and then proceeded to clap off the mud from his boots.

Maggie was on a mission to kill again.

She had dreamt of it for most of the night. Something primal was pulling her in this direction.

Upon entering the covering canopy of the forest, she made her way stealthily through several paths, always sniffing and doing her detective work through her olfactory senses. Once she deemed a location was perfect, she leapt onto a low, thick branch of a cottonwood tree and then laid down to wait.

Maggie wanted to test herself and see if there was a beast in that wild that was her equal. She had killed for self-defense, she had killed to protect, now she wanted to kill to see if she could just for sustenance. Oh sure, she knew Farmer Mills and his wife would never let her go hungry, this was for her own satisfaction and pride.

She was never a violent dog or surly in any sense of the word, be it to humans or other dogs. Obviously if you were a squirrel or a deer you were going to get chased but even Maggie was not sure what she would have done with her prey had she ever caught it.

This new urge to hunt came from somewhere deep within. It came from a place away from society and the world of housebroken canines. This compulsion came from a place of outdoor nights under the stars, hunting in packs, and using all of her senses. For Maggie, this was her time to do the battle of life and to see where she ranked in the vicious circle of living beings and really know if she could thrive in the arena of the survival of the fittest.

She let various woodchucks and mice run by unregarded. They were too little and not worthy of her effort this morning. Maggie was tempted by the sight of a black-footed ferret ,not because of its size but only because she had never witnessed one before. The ferret made its way along the dirt animal highway with its body intact.

Though she slept well the night before Maggie began to doze off as she waited for her appropriate prey. The cool morning was perfect for her thick coat of fur, she was neither too hot nor too cold. Just enough breeze snuck through the trees for her liking as well. The singing of the birds serenaded her as she drifted off to a dream about her Family.

Maggie pictured herself in the kitchen on the morning of the week that her Family dressed up in their best clothes and made a resplendent breakfast. All sorts of colors and manners of scents would abound in that kitchen those mornings. Maggie knew to wait respectfully on the periphery of the culinary action as children and parents went this way and that with their plates and cutlery.

And once everyone was at the table Dr. Fairbanks would walk over to where Maggie sat regally and patiently and the veterinarian would place a large plate of the feast in front of the dog. Dr. Fairbanks would hold up her index finger and Maggie would wait, trembling and drooling, for the signal. Once Dr. Fairbanks lowered her index finger Maggie would lower her great head and devour the contents of that plate. The bacon was her particular favorite but it was all delicious to her.

Bacon.

And that's when Maggie woke up and from her perch on the branch saw the great Eurasian wild boar digging its snout into the dirt for insects. The snorting beast was twice Maggie's weight and three feet in height and five feet in length. It was a male with sharp tusks and a couple of war wounds on its backside. He was a contentious boar who suffered no other competitors for its food. Had a man been standing there on that brush filled animal highway that boar would have probably gored him to death. Maggie wanted to now see if she could be a humans' equal when it came to this forest's version of natural selection. Either way it would be a duel to the death.

***

Once her parents left for work Scott snuck into Dee-Dee's house and began to make her breakfast. He cracked two eggs and then began to beat them while a pan heated up and melted the pat of butter he had placed into it. Scott then went into the cupboard and got out a glass, examined it, saw it was not perfectly clean, and then found one that was. He then poured orange juice into it and put the filled glass into the refrigerator to keep it extra cold and delicious for his true love.

Next he laid down some strips of bacon into a pan and began to move them around with a knife. The sound of the sizzling and the fragrant smells of his handiwork soon wafted its way over to Dee-Dee's bedroom and she awoke from her sleep with a smile. She thought it was strange, but good, that her mother was making such a large breakfast on a workday.

Stretching and yawning she got out of bed and padded her bare feet down the hallway and then shrieked in joy, "Scott!" She ran up to him and hugged him and buried her head into his shoulders. He tried to keep moving the bacon around with his left hand while his right hand held her tight.

"How are you feeling?" Scott asked his petite girlfriend.

"Oh, I'm fine. All this for me?" Dee-Dee gratefully asked and her face nuzzled now into his neck.

"You deserve all this and more," he lovingly replied, being careful not to burn the bacon or the eggs.

"I love you." Dee-Dee said with a kiss to his neck.

"I love you more, sunshine. So did your parents say I can take you to the fair Friday?" Scott asked.

"They kept saying no, but I wore them down. We can go!" Dee-Dee exclaimed and lifted herself up and now kissed Scott's cheek. There was then much more kissing and hugging between the two young lovers before the breakfast was made and consumed.

***

The wild boar smelled Maggie before it ever saw her. It could smell a meal or a rival from seven miles away. The great beast swung its tusks left and right, the swirling wind kept the boar from knowing exactly which direction the scent of another animal was coming from. Maggie was poised on her perch of the cottonwood branch, her large head was lowered and her hind legs were ready to pounce. She bared her teeth but remained quiet and did not let a growl escape her mouth.

The agitated boar snorted and continued its lateral movement still not knowing where the scent of a predator was coming from. As Maggie watched her prey prepare for battle she thought back on the visits she took with Dr. Fairbanks to mend other animals. Maggie was able to witness the birth of calves, foals, kittens, puppies, and piglets. Maggie was never aggressive or antagonistic towards any of these animals or their mothers. Dr. Fairbanks could take Maggie with her on any call and feel secure that her dog would behave appropriately.

Maggie had always been a gentle soul and was not known to initiate an attack on any animal, provided it was not a squirrel or deer. Those two animals were always a green light to her aggression, but that was so deep in her DNA that she could not fight that even if she wanted to.

As Maggie prepared to strike the wild boar she thought specifically on the birth of the piglets. She was taken with their high pitched squealing and the odd way they waddled around the hay. When she wandered over for a closer inspection they were so cute and helpless she actually licked one of the piglets. The mother pig snorted protectively but continued to lay in the hay. Maggie backed up a few paces and continued to observe the scene.

The snort the mother pig gave in Maggie's direction sounded quite similar to the sound the wild boar was making now in the forest. Maggie was no stranger to killing and rather enjoyed the battle. But she had never murdered. She knew this would be murder.

This was not self-defense, or to protect another, or to eat. This was just to kill to see if she could kill. She no longer bared her teeth. Maggie withdrew from her aggressive posture and instead lay back down on the safety of the cottonwood tree branch. The wild boar, even if it could see Maggie, could never reach her from the vantage point. Maggie let the beast thrash for a bit and then after a while it simply vanished down the path from where it came from originally.

Maggie felt good with her decision to not do murder. It was not her. It would never be her. She leapt down from the branch and exited the forest and returned to the farm and the front porch of the house.

Maggie then slept peacefully for the next hour.

***

Barney slept peacefully on his front porch. He had been missing his old friend Maggie as did his Family but as the days stretched into weeks since he saw her the memory began to fade. Aubrey kept hoping Maggie would return but as the month passed she too began to think less about the huge dog that invaded their lives for a brief but joyful time.

***

Farmer Mills awakened Maggie with a "Come on, girl!" command. Maggie raised her great head and then her body and ran over to the pick up truck for another trip into town to the Northern Feed and Grain Store.

As Maggie rode with her whole head out of the window and enjoyed the breeze and the scents that went along with it, Farmer Mills turned the dial on the radio looking for a song he liked. It took awhile but finally a Kenny Rogers song came on and he let it play. The song had come out the year before, it was called 'Through the Years'. As the words were sung Farmer Mills sang along, not really hearing what was being sung.

Maggie enjoyed the sound of his voice as she watched the country-side go by at forty miles an hour. Had she been able to read she would have noticed two more foreclosure signs that went up on two more farms. Then she no longer heard his voice but she did hear him sniffle. 'Through the years, you never let me down.' Maggie then heard a loud sigh of anguish from Farmer Mills and she turned to look at him. 'You turned my life around. The sweetest days I've found, I've found with you, through the years'.

Farmer Mills wiped his eyes on his sleeve and kept on driving.

***

"What is the deal with him?" Jimmy Tarson asked his father in reference to Farmer Mills. The farmer had just left the Northern Feed and Grain store and Jimmy had another unsuccessful bonding attempt with the man.

"You mean Farmer Mills?" Buddy Tarson asked his son as they walked through the gravel parking lot back to their store. They had carried out most of Farmer Mills supplies and then petted his huge dog. A few of the items on the farmer's list were not in stock and Jimmy had considerately offered to drive the supplies out himself when they came in and all he got for his offer was a grunt and a nod from Farmer Mills.

"Yes, why is he so grumpy to me?" Jimmy asked as he held the door open for his father who went directly into his office. Jimmy followed his father.

"Here." Buddy Tarson said after ruffling through his desk and finding a copy of the newspaper he was looking for.

"This is from two years ago." Jimmy said, reading the headline. "I don't see anything about -"

His father pointed to the story below the headline. "There."

Jimmy read the first paragraph. "Oh, dear God!"

***

"Come on honey, let's go, it'll be a fun family trip to get everyone's minds off of, you know." Mr. Fairbanks said to his wife as they were doing their nighttime ablutions.

"But what if someone calls with information on Maggie." Dr. Fairbanks asked with deep concern as she put toothpaste on her toothbrush.

Mr. Fairbanks chose his words carefully and then answered, "Honey, it's been almost two months, I just don't know anymore." He saw the hurt in his wife's eyes. He tried to brighten her mood, "But if someone does call we have that new answering machine. Come on, let's do this for the kids, let's go to the State Fair this weekend!"

From the hallway an excited Giselle chimed in, "Wait, what? We're going to the State Fair? We are? Finally? I've wanted to go for years but no, it's too far, it's too crowded, it's too whatever! Yes, finally, we're going!" Giselle ran in and then out of her parent's bathroom and then down the hall to her brothers' room and excitedly shared the news of the possible trip with them.

***

It was a chore Farmer Mills had dreaded and put off all summer but there was no time left to waste. The lever had to be replaced. There were no two ways around it. He had tried to make himself do it various times over the course of the summer but now that it was harvest time it had to be done.

He gathered his tools and arranged them in his tool box and with Maggie at his side he walked from his work shed over to the silo. His stomach was already in tumult and his face grimaced as his breathing became labored. After two years it was no easier. Why? Why did it have to happen? Why couldn't he have seen it coming? Why did he put all of this in motion? Why did he want to continue to live in this world of pain and such deep rooted sorrow?

He patted Maggie's head more as a way to gather strength for the task at hand than a show of affection. Maggie took it as affection and wagged her tail and got an extra bounce into her walk.

Farmer Mills opened the door to the silo and Maggie eagerly leapt into the round area that would soon be filled with tons of grain, if he could fix the lever. The lever.

Maggie had no idea what the recent history of this silo was, she was just happy to be sniffing around a new place. Farmer Mills bent over his tool box and took out the wrench and then started to stand up straight and turn the bolt that held the lever together. He turned it twice and then sank to his feet and began to sob uncontrollably. First quietly, as was his manner, and then more audibly as he could not control his anguish any longer. Maggie stopped sniffing around and looked at him when she heard his pain. She quickly ran over to him and tried to lick his face but his hands covered it. She then licked his ears. She was scared and nervous and just knew she had to show her care and concern somehow.

Farmer Mills reached out and hugged her and she laid down over his legs and let him continue to hug her and his sobbing endured. He then confessed his sins to the dog.

"Why did I give him the farm? Why?" Farmer Mills asked the dog who stared lovingly back at him and listened. "Why then? Interest rates were sky high! The grain embargo with Russia! It was the worst time ever to own a farm, still is! Why did I do that?"

Maggie tried to lick him when he paused talking but he wouldn't let her.

"I thought it was a wonderful gift, giving Ryne the farm, hoping he and his fiance would have the life Lily and I had on it. Growing crops and growing a family. I put too much pressure on him, at the worst possible time, the economy in the toilet. Too many bills. No hope for a turnaround. Why did I do that?"

Farmer Mills sobbed harder now than before. Maggie was at a loss for what to do for him, she knew he did not want to be licked. So she simply put her head on his lap as he sat on the dirt ground of the silo. The silo.

***

"So his son died from..." Jimmy asked his father as he put the newspaper down on the desk. Buddy sat down in his comfortable leather chair and Jimmy sat opposite his father in a less comfy chair.

"There is no official consensus on that. Oh, they know he died of asphyxiation, but they don't know for sure it was suicide, or if it was an accident." Buddy answered his son. Buddy could not imagine losing Jimmy in that way, or any way.

"To have all of those tons of grain drop on him like that, in that silo, it had to be suicide, right? Weren't they having problems with the mortgage?"

"Most of the farms are, especially then. Actually, it's not much better now, either. But then it was really bad. Yes, how else do you explain, you know, how it happened. Who else would have pulled that lever?"

"But Dad, I mean, couldn't he have asked for a loan, or help, or something?" Jimmy asked his father.

"He was a really sweet kid, a handsome young man. Very nice manners. Always wanted to help, didn't want to be a burden. Probably felt now that his parents were retired he didn't want to burden them. Then things kept getting worse and worse. He was a good farmer but look at how many farms have been foreclosed in the past two years. Felt like if he was gone, and insurance paid out, then maybe they'd be alright. That's my thought on it, that he took his own life in that silo to not further burden his parents."

"But poor Farmer Mills is distraught, he looks like a walking corpse himself. There is no joy or life to him."

"He's changed, that's for sure. He used to be the nicest man, very friendly, very talky, now, good luck getting more than a sentence out of him. It's like a part of his heart and his soul have been cut out."

"Is there anything we can do for him? Is there anything anyone can do for him? I mean, you raised us Christian, I want to help him. But, I just don't know how to, or if anyone could help him." Jimmy said, his eyes welling up with tears.

Buddy Tarson saw the raw emotion in his son's eyes. He also tried to imagine how he would be if what happened to Farmer Mills' son happened to his son. Tears began to well in the older man's eyes as well. "We can pray for him, son. We can keep trying to be there for him if he ever needs us, or anything."

"It doesn't seem like enough though, Dad."

"It's all we have, son."

***

Lily searched the grounds of their farm for her husband and found neither him nor Maggie. She had a serene feeling knowing that Maggie was with him, and never left his side. She somehow felt safer knowing that dog was so attached to her husband.

She checked the south fence where he was working the week before and when he was not there she checked his work shed. The tool box was gone so she knew he was working somewhere, but where? Most, if not all, of the chores had been finished. It had been a very productive summer. The only big chore left was to fix that lever in the silo.

The silo.

She stood still in the work shed as a chill ran over her entire body and her heart felt like it was being squeezed. She had to work to breathe. She did not know she was crying until the tears ran down her cheeks and onto her neck. She had never been an overly emotional woman until two summers ago. Now, she rarely had her emotions in check. She could watch a commercial that had a blonde haired boy and her heart would crumble thinking about her dear, sweet boy who was now gone. Gone forever.

And then she started to run to the silo because she knew that was where her husband must be and she was very scared. Lily ran across the dirt driveway and over the little wooden bridge her husband and son had built together a decade ago. There were so many tears falling from her eyes she could barely see the way to the silo.

Lily ran into the building and then took a quick right hand turn and then saw the doorway to the silo. She stopped, scared at what she might find but at the same time she had to hurry in and see for herself. She wanted to call out her husband's name but the words would not come so instead she darted to the doorway and looked into the silo.

She saw her husband still sitting on the ground that was mixed with dirt, some hay, and a few grain particles. Maggie was sitting protectively on his legs.

Farmer Mills looked up at his wife and smiled! Actually smiled! "I'm all cried out." He said and kind of laughed.

She was shocked, that was not the response she was expecting. "What? Deary, what, are you ok?"

"Lily, my love, I think I am." He said, smiling still, and patted the ground next to him for her to sit. She did, still confused and nervous.

"Are you sure you're ok?" Lily asked again once she was seated.

"I really think I am. I haven't been in here, in this silo, since, since a while ago."

"I know, Deary." Lily said as her tears streamed down her face again at the hurt she knew her husband felt.

"Like I said, I'm all cried out." Farmer Mills then looked at his wife and her grief stricken wet cheeks, "But I can see you're not." Farmer Mills laughed again. Lily had just heard him laugh more times in the last two minutes than he had in the previous two years!

"Deary -"

"I'll explain. It's all my fault, all of it." Farmer Mills' wife tried to interrupt him and absolve him of the guilt but he would not hear of it. "It is, I'm solely guilty, it was my idea, I gave him the farm at the worst economic time in our country's history for farming. I did that. All this time I've been walking around with the grief but not acknowledging the guilt. Now that I have the guilt, I have a responsibility to the world. He was the sweetest, such a gentle giant, and now he is gone and the world is poorer for that fact. And it is my fault, so I need to make it right with the world. I need to be happy, and to help others, and to be kind, not walk around depressed and angry. I need to honor Ryne's memory. And I can't do that feeling sorry for myself, especially when it's all my fault."

"Deary, it is not your fault -"

"Lily, my love, let's not argue, this is a good thing. One hundred percent of this is my fault and I don't want to fight you, I want to hug you, and dance with you, and make you happy. Because you deserve happiness after what I caused. You, and all of Nebraska, heck, all of the world deserves happiness and it is my mission to provide it. What did all of Ryne's friends and classmates say about him? That if they were ever feeling alone, or sitting alone at lunch, or anything like that, they always knew he'd sit with them or talk with them. He'd always be a friend they could count on. I need to be a friend that everyone can count on. You know who taught me all of this?"

Lily shook her head, "Deary?"

"This dog, here. All she does is serve, and protect, and love. All this furry giant does is make people happy and give of herself. What does she ask? A scratch behind the ears? If I was half the great human she is..." His voice trailed off and he scratched Maggie behind the ears and her tail wagged as she laid there.

"Deary, you learned all of this from a dog we just met last month?"

"Yes I did. And shame on me for taking so long to learn. What a grump I've been! A selfish grump! But no more!"

"No more?"

"Time is precious. I cannot waste anymore of it." Farmer Mills put his arms around his arm and with the other arm he continued to scratch Maggie behind her ears. Her wagging tail caused some dirt to kick up and float away.

***

"No, Dad, I'm serious, he hugged me!" Jimmy Tarson exclaimed as after he burst into his father's office at the Northern Feed and Grain Store. He had just come back from delivering a few of the supplies to Farmer Mills that were restocked at the store.

"Hugged you?" Buddy Tarson asked in disbelief.

"Hugged me! Yes. As God is my witness, I swear Farmer Mills did."

"So what did you do?"

Jimmy looked at his father like he was just asked the silliest question ever and then basically shouted, "I hugged him back of course!"

***

The Nebraska State Fair was in full bloom on that sunny Saturday as temperatures reached back into the eighties after a dip into the sixties the previous week. Summer wanted one more show of its strength before succumbing to Fall. There were rides, carnival attractions, games, animals, and of course a pie baking contest to enjoy.

As Gracie Moore flew over the vast acres of the State Fair she was struck by how much bigger it was than any of the county fairs she had performed at the previous couple of months. It usually took her a few seconds to fly over the area of a county fair but this State Fair just seemed to go on and on! The number of people and their cars in the various parking lots added to the actual fairgrounds themselves made for an impressive display.

It was on her second fly over of the grandstand, at a height of only a hundred feet so as to attract attention to her plane and the show she was to put on later in the day, that she noticed something that caught her eyes. She made another pass, this one a little lower, and then did a barrel roll and flew once more over the same area. That third pass is when she was sure of what she had seen.

Gracie Moore immediately landed her bright yellow bi-plane on the makeshift dirt runway and then ran off in the direction of what captured her fancy.

***

Sheriff Rawley was walking slowly through the midway while balancing four hotdogs that he had pilfered in his arms. He walked along, Sidekick Pete was no longer his sidekick, not after the incident at the stream. That gave Pete the courage to break free. Sheriff Rawley's attention was focused on his ill gotten lunch when he noticed a beautiful blonde woman trot by. He looked up and squinted and saw that it was the pilot, Gracie Moore. Sheriff picked up his pace so as to follow her. He enjoyed the view of her from the rear as much as the front.

As he increased his speed his stolen food jostled in his grip but he did not drop them. He then saw the pretty pilot stop by an older man and his large, mostly black colored dog. Sheriff concentrated on Gracie Moore as she bent over slightly to pet the dog. His eyes really never made it to the dog.

"I know this dog!" Gracie Moore said to the older man that held the dog's leash. She petted the dog under her chin. "This is Maggie!"

Farmer Mills smiled brightly at the beautiful young woman and exclaimed, "So that's this girl's name! Wait, is she your dog?"

"No, no, I wish! She is a doll!" Gracie said upon which Maggie laid down on her side and accepted all the affection she could. "No, I met her a month or so back when my plane had trouble and I had to land in a field. She was with these two teenagers, but they didn't know where she came from either."

"Really? How interesting." Farmer Mills replied.

"So how did you come to have her?" Gracie asked, still petting Maggie. But then Maggie abruptly rose up from her laying position and barked and then bared her teeth in the direction behind Gracie.

Both Farmer Mills and Gracie were shocked at this behavior until they saw the man behind Gracie that was the cause of Maggie's display of aggression.

When Maggie rose and barked her warning, Sheriff finally noticed who the dog was that the pretty pilot was petting and he was so frightened that he dropped all four of his hot dogs onto the ground.

"Him!" Farmer Mills said in an angry voice to Gracie. "I got Maggie from him when he showed me he didn't deserve her!"

Sheriff Rawley did not hesitate to speak or be spoken to any longer and turned tail and ran off in the opposite direction of the massive Newfie/Shepherd mix.

"Go ahead girl, they're yours now." Farmer Mills said and Maggie walked up and gobbled the four hotdogs down her prodigious throat. Farmer Mills filled Gracie Moore into the complete backstory of how he found her in the ditch with those two carnies.

When Maggie finished her snack they all walked together to the runway because Farmer Mills wanted to see Gracie Moore's vintage bi-plane. As they approached the plane they saw two teenagers standing near it.

"No way!" Gracie said as they got closer to her plane. "You two?"

"Gracie!" Dee-Dee yelled and ran over to hug the pilot. Her boyfriend Scott waited back by the plane while the two women hugged.

"How is, um, everything?" Gracie whispered into Dee-Dee's ear.

"Oh, just fine! I'm not, you know, I'm not pregnant after all! It, uh, it finally came!!" Dee-Dee whispered back excitedly.

"I am so happy for you, for you both! Someday, sure, but not when you're fifteen, right?" Gracie said, still hugging the young girl.

"Right!" Dee-Dee agreed and then introductions were made with Farmer Mills and Maggie was once again petted and fawned over and she basked in all the attention. "Scott and I saw your plane fly over and we knew it was you and we just had to see you again!" Dee-Dee explained.

Though gaps were filled in with Maggie's story thanks to the appearance of Gracie Moore and the two teenage lovers there was still no answer to who or where her owners were located. They all talked and caught up until Gracie had to get her plane ready for the air show she had to put on that afternoon.

As her plane took off and she looked down she could see Scott giving Dee-Dee a piggyback ride while Farmer Mills walked Maggie over to the stage where the pie baking contest was being judged.

***

The car ride over to the State Fair for the Fairbanks' had been tense as Dr. Fairbanks got into an argument with Julian over his insistence on being a farmer.

"All I'm saying," Dr. Fairbanks told her eldest son, "is while we're at the fair we could pop over to the university for a nice college visit."

"But I still have yet to decide if I even want to go to college!" Julian heatedly retorted to his mother.

"Julian." His father cautioned him over his tone.

"Why can't I just do what I want to do with my life?" Julian wondered and his mother did not have a good answer to that question so she just let it be. They rode on to the State Fair in silence.

***

A seventh place finish in the pie baking contest for Lily left her beaming. The competition was large and accomplished. There were over one hundred entries from all over the state of Nebraska. "That puts you in the top ten percent of the entire state!" Farmer Mills joyously exclaimed as he hugged his proud wife. He examined the blue ribbon that she won and was pinned to her blouse. "Only the top ten got a blue ribbon in the whole state! Congrats, Lily my love!"

"Deary." Lily said embarrassed.

A little girl of about eleven came up to the farmer and his wife. Her mother had entered the pie baking contest but was not among the top ten bakers. But the pie contest was not what she was interested in. Her parents were looking for her and calling out her name but she could only think of one thing.

"Maggie!" She exclaimed and the dog turned to her and excitedly wagged her tail. "Maggie" Aubrey said again and petted the dog.

"Everyone here seems to know this dog!" Farmer Mills said to his wife. "Is she your dog?" He asked the little girl as she hugged and petted Maggie.

"She was for a couple of days." Aubrey explained and then was joined by her frantic parents who finally located her.

The farmer and his wife were then able to piece together another part of Maggie's journey but there still was no clue on who her original family was or where they were located.

***

The car ride for the Fairbanks family went from surly silence to a screaming match between oldest son and mother with the father trying to play peacemaker and the two other children too stunned to say or do anything. Dr. Fairbanks just could not let go of her aversion to Julian not wanting a college education. Logic went out the window as her anger got the better of her

And she yelled to her eldest son, "You are too smart to be so stupid as to this unintelligent choice!"

"Mom, I honestly have no clue what you just meant!"

"You are going to college! That's final!" Dr. Fairbanks declared as they exited the car in the State Fair parking lot.

"I'm an adult, what are you going to do? Drag me there?" Julian asked.

"If I have to!" Dr. Fairbanks yelled while her husband tried to calm her down by patting her back softly. "And don't pat my back!" She screamed to her husband who then recoiled his touch from her.

"I'm going to find Gianna!" Julian said and started to storm off.

"Gianna? What is your girlfriend doing here?" Dr. Fairbanks asked disgustedly.

"Oh, I don't know, it's the State Fair, what do you think she's doing here? She came with a few friends, I'm going to find them and hang."

Before his wife could yell something else at their son her husband interceded. "Ok, son, you find them and we'll meet up later at the huge butter sculpture, maybe around eight o'clock? Does that work?"

"Sure, dad, sure." Julian said with an appreciative tone. "Bye guys, have fun today." Julian said to his little sister and brother. "Bye mom." Julian said to his mother and then turned and walked away.

Dr. Fairbanks paused and then called out to him, "Bye son!" He raised his hand and waved but never broke stride.

***

One of Gracie Moore's duties as a pilot beside her stunt flying shows was to also pull long banners behind her plane with an advertisement. Some might be for a local restaurant and bar, some might be for the services of a prominent lawyer. When she landed after pulling one of these banners behind her plane as she flew all over the area she got an idea and talked to her ground crew about it. Before dusk they were able to get the banner finished to her liking.

***

At eight o'clock Julian and Gianna met up with his family at the huge butter sculpture. Dr. Fairbanks tried but could not extend a warm greeting to Julian's girlfriend, it was tepid at best. "Hello, Gianna."

"Hello Dr. Fairbanks." Gianna replied, more than a little intimidated. Julian had filled her in on everything his mother said and demanded.

"Where are your friends? I thought you were here with friends?" Dr. Fairbanks asked the girl in an accusatory tone.

Julian intervened to defend his girlfriend, "She is here with friends, mom, they're getting some food. Did you think I lied?"

And the conversation downwardly escalated from there. Things were said, and shouted, that they both later regretted.

After too many minutes of this Julian declared, "I'm going to go home with Gianna! I'll see you later tonight, maybe." And before his mother could get out a complete sentence he stormed off.

She ordered her son back but he did not obey and grabbed his girlfriend's hand and kept walking away.

Dr. Fairbanks declared the day a disaster and gathered up the rest of her family and they all left the fair as the sun started to set.

In the distance they heard an old fashioned bi-plane warming up it's engine right before take off.

As Gracie Moore took off the banner unfurled and the message was clear to anybody still at the fair and looking upwards: Please call if you have info on a large Newfie/Shepherd mix dog Maggie 555-536-3654.

Neither Dr. Fairbanks nor any of the members of her family that were with her saw the banner, they were already in their car headed back to home.

As Farmer Mills and his wife Lily looked to the sky and saw the yellow bi-plane fly by with that message they had mixed feelings. Sure, they wanted to do the right thing and reunite Maggie with her family but at the same time, selfishly, they did not want to lose her. She had become a dear member of their family. She had become an instrument of healing. If they were being honest, Farmer Mills and his wife Lily had to admit that they needed that loveable and sweet dog.

As Dee-Dee and Scott looked skyward they also hoped Maggie would be reunited with her family. They also vowed that in a couple of years when they got married they would get a big adorable dog just like her. And then children shortly after that. But not yet, not when they were still so young.

***

Audrey and her family also saw the banner and thought it was a great idea that just might result in a happy ending for the gentle giant of a dog that made quite an impression on them in the few short days Maggie spent on their farm.

Gracie Moore flew on in the fading light of the day and marveled at the amount of cars that were already driving away from the fair on the highway. Their headlights made a parade of illumination for miles.

MAY 1983

Mrs. Kang drove off from the Fairbanks property with her truck filled with three puppies. On the surface it had been a wonderful business transaction but it was so much more than that for both parties.

Once Mrs. Kang left with her furry treasures, Mr. and Dr. Fairbanks loaded their pick up trucks with bags of dog food. Julian carried two suitcases while Giselle and Freddie kept watch over their own furry treasures. The puppies were an indispensable part of the healing process for all the parties involved.

Life without Maggie had taught the Fairbanks family about the importance of family and of time spent wisely. The old adage 'you don't know what you have until it's gone' rang so true for the Fairbanks'. They just always assumed Maggie would be there in their backyard waiting for them. They just always assumed they would all be there in that house, always. But time marches on, people change, children grow up and leave.

Once all the animals were loaded into each of the two trucks the journey started. Depending on traffic it would not take more than an hour, but for some of them, it would be a world away. A world that could never again truly come back to.

As they drove past farms, some still vibrant and thriving, most not, a feeling of melancholy overwhelmed them all. Winter was over and though Spring and its rebirth were upon the land the Fairbanks family knew this moment was bittersweet. It was a long time coming but it still felt like it got here too soon.

And then just like that the first truck put on it's turn signal and the second truck followed suit. As the two trucks pulled into the farm and drove the winding dirt driveway up to the farm house Dr. Fairbanks gulped back a wave of emotions that were drowning her. Her husband Joseph grabbed her hand and squeezed it. She felt better but still wished she could reset the clock back a year, maybe many years, at least a decade. Why did life speed by so quickly?

Both trucks parked and the people in them got out. The children looked around and saw the corn stalks just coming out of the ground and the tall silo that had a newly painted American flag on it, and then they saw the couple coming off of their porch to greet them.

"Welcome! Welcome!" Farmer Mills warmly said and opened his arms to hug whoever was closest to him, which just happened to be Giselle. After hugging her he hugged Dr. Fairbanks, and then Freddie, and then Mr. Fairbanks, and then Gianna. Lily was busy hugging Julian and then made sure she wrapped her arms around all the rest of them.

All that time, during all the greetings and hugging and hellos, Maggie was running from one person to the next, getting her fair share of affection. She hadn't been to this farm since the previous Fall and was excited to see Farmer Mills and his wife as they were to see her.

Everything happens for a reason.

Julian and Gianna remained at the State Fair that night in September and saw the banner behind Gracie Moore's bi-plane, and called, and Maggie was reunited with her Family the next day. Mrs. Kang was the second call Dr. Fairbanks made that day. Many months later three of Maggie's puppies went home with Mrs. Kang, two were staying with the Fairbanks, and the biggest male was going to Farmer Mills and his wife Lily.

When Giselle held up the puppy that was for Farmer Mills and his wife the older couple smiled and let out a collective "Ahhhh."

"He looks like a Duke!" Lily stated and thus that became the puppies' name.

"So Duke he is!" Farmer Mills decreed. He then pointed to his farm house and told Julian, "Go ahead and put your things in your room. I have a lot to teach you!"

Farmer Mills would teach Julian everything the great man knew about farming and that young man and his fiance Gianna, along with Duke, would keep that couple from ever being lonely that wonderful summer. The corn grew tall, the boy ate lavishly thanks to the hands of Lily, and knowledge was passed down lovingly. Gianna and Dr. Fairbanks stood with their arms around each other as a detente was achieved. Maggie could not decide who to lick next.

After that summer Julian would go off to college to learn about farming from professors and then continue to return each summer to Farmer Mills and his wife Lily to both help and absorb.

Maggie felt very proud. It was her adventurous spirit, along with a snorting deer and an unlatched gate, that caused all of those dominos to fall into place. Maggie wondered how much good would come from her next adventure.